"Now, where were we before I left you all alone in the dark?"

He placed two fingers under Kacey's chin.

"Right about here," Kacey replied, pressing her body to his, not about to erect any barriers that would interfere with the raw, sexual awakening he'd stirred inside of her. Though shocked by the intensity of her need to be near him, she loved the sensation of isolation and privacy that descended on her as she stood in his arms.

Between the slow kisses that he placed on her exposed skin, his hands crept downward, moving along her spine until they clasped her buttocks in a firm caress and crushed her soft womanhood against his rigid sex, fusing them together like two pattern pieces perfectly joined at the seam.

Succumbing to his tantalizing move, Kacey opened her mouth and took his tongue deep into her mouth, letting his languid thrusts satisfy a thirst for Leon Archer that she felt might never be quenched.

Books by Anita Bunkley

Kimani Romance

Suite Embrace
Suite Temptation
Spotlight on Desire
Vote for Love
First Class Seduction
Boardroom Seduction

ANITA BUNKLEY

is the author of many successful mainstream novels and novellas and is enjoys writing romance for her many fans. A member of the Texas Institute of Letters and an NAACP Image Award nominee, she is the recipient of a 2007 Career Achievement Award from *RT Book Reviews*. Anita lives in Houston, Texas, with her husband, Crawford.

Boardroom SEDUCTION

ANITA BUNKLEY

KIMANI™
ROMANCE

To my husband, Crawford, with love.

KIMANI PRESS™

ISBN-13: 978-0-373-86193-4

BOARDROOM SEDUCTION

Recycling programs for this product may not exist in your area.

www.kimanipress.com

Printed in U.S.A.

Dear Reader,

Living on the Texas Gulf coast means lots of sunshine, extremely hot summers and, of course, opportunities to swim nearly year round. However, I am originally from Ohio, where the winters are long and the summers are short, so I have experienced, and enjoyed, living in both climates. My inspiration for *Boardroom Seduction* is centered on the many differences between the urban East Coast lifestyle and the more relaxed Texas way of life, and how such differences impact a romantic relationship.

While preparing for this story, I thought about my own experiences when I first arrived in the Houston area. As I began to explore the unusual, wonderful aspects of the Texas coast, I fell in love with the climate, the food, the outdoor lifestyle and, of course, the people. Swimsuits are a big part of a woman's wardrobe in this sun-splashed climate, so what better occupation for my heroine than a swimsuit designer? And so Kacey Parker was born!

As you travel between New York and Texas with Kacey and Leon, I hope you will feel the pain of their dilemma as they test their abilities to accept new worlds and learn to appreciate each other's choices.

I hope you enjoy my fun-in-the-sun romance as we cross geographical borders and watch love blossom between two very talented and devoted characters.

Enjoy! If you want to drop me a line, please email me at arbun@sbcglobal.net.

Read with love!

Anita Bunkley

Chapter 1

"And finally, here's my showstopper. I call this one Sheer Double Dip," Kacey Parker announced with pride, moving to stand beside the final photo in her PowerPoint presentation. She clicked the remote control and sent the image of a leggy model in a hot pink monokini and a dazzling bronze tan onto the screen. When the sultry image emerged, gasps of approval erupted from the two people seated at the conference table at Leeman's Retailers, Inc.

"This is the only swimsuit in my SunKissed line that looks totally natural when dry, but becomes sexily opaque when wet," Kacey went on, sliding her gaze toward Steve Hadley, eager to catch her boss's reaction.

At least he isn't frowning, and that's good, Kacey decided, hopeful that she had impressed him enough to green-light her swimsuit designs for his chain of department stores.

"Hmm, see-through fabric?" Ariana Mendio, the vice president of merchandising for the upscale department store, murmured. "That'll make for some stunning surprises when the ladies get out of the water," she noted in her well-modulated Italian accent.

Kacey smiled in agreement, happy to have Ariana, who'd been with Leeman's for eighteen years, on her side. The woman was an absolute fixture at the company and her opinion carried weight.

"Surprises? Absolutely," Kacey agreed with a nod in Ariana's direction. "The fabric is a new synthetic that designers are calling Naughty Net. It's soft, durable and becomes extremely sheer when water hits it."

Kacey took a deep breath, pleased, so far, with her presentation. She'd joined Leeman's as a sales clerk eight years ago, and her warm personality and flair for design had helped her move into the position of director of special promotions. In that job, she'd gained valuable knowledge about what buyers wanted, expected and would pay dearly for. A competitive swimmer in college, Kacey especially loved working on promotional events in women's sportswear and swimwear, where she enjoyed pulling together dramatic displays of the functional yet attractive apparel that drew customers' attention.

However, as fulfilling and demanding as her current job was, once she left the store, she dedicated herself to her dream job—becoming a swimsuit designer. Over the past year she created her portfolio and when she showed it to Ariana, her coworker immediately took it directly to Steve Hadley, who was so impressed, he invited Kacey to show him more of what she could do.

"Is this fabric readily available?" Steve asked, jotting notes in the margins of Kacey's portfolio.

"Right now, only from China," she answered, wishing she had better news. "But it makes this one-piece the sexiest swimsuit any woman could ever want. Just look at the detail. The plunging neckline, low scooped back and high-cut legs."

"Specialty fabrics could add thousands to production costs," he mused as he flipped through Kacey's proposal, a slight frown bridging his thick black eyebrows.

Kacey paused, inhaled and swallowed her apprehension, aware that her specs related to costs and materials would require a significant financial commitment at a time when upscale stores like Leeman's were nervously watching the bottom line.

"I know," she agreed. "However, I'm hoping to find better rates per unit in Thailand," she acknowledged, setting aside her remote control. "I'm sourcing that now."

Finished with her presentation, Kacey walked to the far side of the room and turned up the lights, allowing the Manhattan skyline to loom dark and gray in the expanse of glass windows that made up one wall. Kacey squinted at the heavy April rain pounding the buildings and slicking the skyline, weary of the thunderstorm that had started during the night and continued to rage. She was definitely not looking forward to a crowded train ride home to Harlem later in the day.

After taking a seat at the conference table across from her boss, Kacey looked directly at Steve Hadley, prepared to expand her pitch. "I know the specialty fabric could run up production costs, but the expense would pay off in the end. Using Naughty Net on the Sheer Double Dip would make it an instant bestseller."

"I love it," Ariana cut in, cooing her words in her sexy Italian voice as she slipped her fingers through a mass of white-blond, shoulder-length hair. Even though she'd lived in America for thirty years and was a naturalized citizen, Ariana took care to maintain her accent, which she laid on thick to dramatic effect when she wanted to make a point. "I adore all eight styles. Great line, Kacey. Wonderful photos. Linette pulled off some very attractive shots."

"Right. Linette is the best," Kacey agreed, referring to Linette Grier, Kacey's best friend and an up-and-coming photographer specializing in sportswear photos. "She's been so busy lately, I was lucky to get her."

"Ah, well, I'm glad you did," Ariana said. "Very nice. Well, Kacey, all I can say is that your designs are spot-on," she continued. "I especially like Twisted Bliss, the black one-piece that shows off just the right amount of skin but still offers full bottom coverage. Excellent choice for, uh…mature women who still keep in shape, shall we say?" She chuckled, winking at Kacey before turning her attention to Steve Hadley. "Older women with disposable cash are our most important demographic, right?"

Hadley inclined his head in brief acknowledgment of Ariana's point. "Kacey, I think your designs show promise and the line is worth exploring," he stated, choosing his words very carefully, without conveying his decision. "However, because you're an employee at Leeman's, it makes for a bit of a sticky situation."

"Conflict of interest, and all that?" Kacey injected.

Steve nodded at Kacey before going on. "Right. You'd

have to leave Leeman's and become a contractor if we decide to proceed with this. But first, let's get some samples made and assess the project, okay?"

"Whatever will work, " Kacey rushed to say, willing to do anything necessary to move her career as a swimsuit designer forward. After all, her goal was much larger than to simply do custom work for one retail outlet. She wanted to have her own design firm, have control of her future, and launch a creative explosion that would make hers a household name.

"However," Steve was saying, "We must source that specialty fabric at a much better price to make the investment pay off." He licked his lower lip in thought, his eyes riveted on the scantily clad model whose image still filled the screen. "I'm thinking that a totally domestic production would be the best option. Save shipping costs and time."

"I agree," Kacey replied, encouraged by the fact that he was leaning toward carrying SunKissed by Kacey in his fourteen Leeman's stores. All he needed was reassurance that the product would turn a profit.

"What about manufacturing in Mexico?" Ariana offered.

With a shift, Kacey smoothed the skirt of her burgundy power suit, crossed her arms and placed them on the table. Leaning toward her coworker, she made a slight grimace of concern. "I checked out a few south-of-the-border plants, but didn't have much luck. However, there are two manufacturers I'm still looking into."

"Kacey," Steve started, clearing his throat. "I want to be clear. I agreed to take a look at your collection because I think you have a good eye for what women want. You also have a great sense of style and I like your swimsuits very much."

Kacey beamed her thanks, but said nothing, holding her breath as Hadley continued.

"But," he went on, "I have concerns about the timing. It's very late into the spring shopping season to introduce a new line of swimwear."

"But women buy swimsuits year-round," Kacey countered, pushing tendrils of highlighted bangs away from her face, now wishing she'd had her spiral curls trimmed during yesterday's visit to the salon. However, she'd been in a rush to get out of the beauty shop and home to put the finishing touches on today's presentation, which it seemed, so far, was going pretty well.

"Exactly," Ariana, stated, agreeing with Kacey about year-round swimsuit purchases. "Winter cruises to the tropics, heated pools in homes and hotels, hot tubs in private residences. That's what keeps women buying swimwear through all the seasons. I know we're getting a late start, Steve, but if we can source the Naughty Net and include the Sheer Double Dip style, I think SunKissed by Kacey could be flying out of our stores in six weeks."

"Hmm," Steve murmured, fingers laced and tented in thought. "Only if we could get fast turnaround on production." He shifted his body to focus on Ariana. "What about Archer Industries? We've worked with them before and always had good results," he remarked. "What do you think?"

"Good possibility," Ariana agreed. "The Archer factory has a reputation for fast turnarounds, high-quality production and cost-effective shipping. They handle quite a few private labels."

"Old man Archer came through with that rare Hawaiian print we needed for the menswear line last year," Steve added.

"Yeah, and saved us a ton of money, too," Ariana agreed.

With a lift of her finger, Kacey joined in. "You're referring to Archer Industries in Texas, right?"

"Yes," Hadley replied. "Rockport. On the Gulf Coast. Not much else is there but the Archer factory. That family has been in business for years. The founder, Leon Archer, is getting on in years, but he runs that shop like a well-oiled machine. He's a dying breed…a good old-fashioned businessman who takes pride in doing a first class job, no matter how large or small."

"I phoned and sent an email to Archer," Kacey said, eager to let her boss know that she'd already considered the family-owned firm that had done quite a bit of business with Leeman's over the years. "I just received an email this morning to contact Nona James, the quality control manager. I'm going to call her as soon as we finish here." Kacey began to gather the papers she'd strewn over the conference table, anxious to return to her office, get on her computer and tie up all the loose ends related to her proposal.

"Don't bother with that," Steve stated. "Mr. Archer deserves a personal call from me. He's a throwback to the old days…likes to do business with the person in charge. In fact, I'll call him right now."

Kacey watched as Steve reached for his handheld, scrolled through his address book and punched in a number. Within seconds he was talking to Mr. Archer, giving the manufacturer an overview of Kacey's proposed swimsuit line.

"Sure, sure," Steve agreed in an expansive voice after several minutes of conversation. "The designer, Kacey Parker, can come down, meet with you and we'll go from there." He turned to Kacey, placing a hand over his phone as he whispered, "He thinks he can do it. And he would like to meet with you at the plant tomorrow afternoon. Go ahead and book a flight to Rockport," he said before returning his attention to his conversation.

"You'll have to fly into Corpus Christi…the closest big city," Ariana offered in a hushed tone. "Rent a car. The factory is on the outskirts of town. About half an hour from the airport."

Kacey nodded, grabbed a pen and began to jot down the instructions that Ariana was giving her while Steve ended his call.

Once he had finished and refocused on Kacey, he told her, "Take your portfolio, fabric samples and proposal to Texas and sell this line to Archer. He's the man we want."

Kacey grinned, drew in a gasp of surprise and then sighed. Had her boss actually given her the green light on her proposal? Was SunKissed by Kacey going to become a reality after so many months of dreaming and planning? She pushed back her chair and stood, papers clutched in one hand, her heartbeat increasing by the second.

"Then, you're saying, it's a go?" she prompted, needing to hear the words from Steve Hadley himself that her swimsuit line was headed into production.

"Yes, it's a tentative go. And if you manage a five percent reduction in overall manufacturing costs, there'll be a nice cash bonus in it for you," he offered, sounding strongly supportive of Kacey's project.

"Oh, I'm sure I can do that, Mr. Hadley. Five percent won't be a problem. Trust me. I'll work this out."

"I hope so. I'm impressed with your designs, Kacey, and if we can have product in stock by mid-June, I feel confident our customers will buy it."

Kacey struggled to appear calm, though she was desperate to scream with joy. She'd been dreaming about this day ever since she started her career in retail merchandising. Now, she had a real shot at shifting her focus toward designing for the masses instead of setting up displays and running in-store contests. She could hardly wait to start the journey.

While Kacey headed toward the conference room door, Steve remained seated, looking over his eyeglasses at her as he advised, "Pack well. You might be in Texas for a while."

"A while?" Kacey quipped, arching a shapely brown eyebrow in his direction. "Certainly Mr. Archer and I can accomplish all we need to do in a day. Two at the most."

"No, if all goes well, I want you to stick around there."

Kacey glanced suspiciously at her boss. "For how long?"

"For as long as it'll take to get SunKissed by Kacey into my stores. No need to rush back here, only to fly back and forth every few weeks," Hadley explained. "I know old man Archer will do his best to accommodate our time frame, but since this is such a rush job, and a risky midseason production as well, we can't afford any mistakes. He and I will iron out the contract details before you get there. I want you to stay close, oversee production and ensure an on-time delivery."

Kacey assessed Steve Hadley with dread in her heart, doubting he understood the enormity of what he was asking of her. Leaving New York City to spend God knows how long in rural Texas was not something she looked forward to. What in the world would she do for fun in a tiny Gulf Coast town with an old man as her business contact?

Suffer in silence, she guessed, prepared to sacrifice the lifestyle she loved to see her designs come to life.

Chapter 2

Back in her cubicle, Kacey immediately booked her flight to Corpus Christi, reserved a rental car and then phoned her friend Linette to share her good news. However, all Kacey got was the photographer's voice mail, so she left a message for Linette to call her back as soon as possible, adding that she had exciting news to share.

That ought to get her attention, Kacey thought as she ended the connection. It was always difficult to reach Linette, who was constantly on the move as she traveled from one location shoot to another. Sometimes it took a week for them to finally catch up with each other due to their busy, on-the-go lifestyles.

Taking a moment to reflect on the impact of her presentation, Kacey pondered the future, a ripple of excitement feathering her insides. She'd begun working on her designs last year, using computer-assisted design (CAD) software that turned her detailed sketches into actual computer drawings. Printed pattern pieces placed on swaths of bold-colored fabric quickly morphed into the samples that she had personally sewn and fitted on models for Linette to photograph. And now, at last, Hadley was giving her the opportunity to create sexy, stylish swimwear that she knew customers would be thrilled to wear.

Hadley was damn sure impressed and Ariana is totally behind me, Kacey mused in satisfaction, realizing how much support she had at Leeman's. If SunKissed by Kacey became the runaway hit she expected, her position with the chic retailer would open doors to all the exclusive shops on Rodeo Drive, as well as retailers like Bergdorf's, Saks, and Neiman's.

A competitive swimmer in college, Kacey loved challenges and loved to win. She knew her petite stature, flawless mocha skin and the thick brown hair that framed her face in curly tendrils made her look a lot younger and less savvy than she was. But at thirty-one, she had made plenty of hard decisions in her drive to become successful, and knew exactly where she wanted to go.

For more than a year, Kacey had labored over her drawing boards, studied the competition and focused on coming up with swimwear that would make such an impact on the marketplace that every retailer would clamor for her swimsuits. Even though the rights to her special label would belong to Leeman's, Kacey knew the professional credit and boost in her fledgling design career were more than she'd ever dreamed of.

Leaving her computer, she went to stand at the large

window behind her desk. Looking out, she swept her gaze over the towering buildings pressed together in midtown Manhattan. The steady rain continued to slick the traffic-clogged streets as dull gray clouds hovered above the tops of skyscrapers. She placed her palm against the glass and shivered. *Too damn cold,* she thought with a shudder, but that's the way it could be in early April in New York. There'd even been a snow flurry last week, but she prayed that warm weather was on the way.

In the foggy distance, Kacey could barely discern the outline of the building where she hoped to live one day. Four blocks from Leeman's, the newly renovated 780-square-foot apartment she dreamed about would be a vast improvement over the tiny closetlike studio in Harlem where she lived now. She'd been saving for two years to make the move, and now, if all went well, her SunKissed line would provide a much-needed boost in her income, allowing her to lease the new apartment in midtown.

But first, she had to go to Texas, get her designs into production, then into stores. And as much as she dreaded an extended stay in a small town like Rockport, she knew the trip would be a welcome break from the damp cold of the city.

"I've got to remain positive," she murmured, deciding to treat her trip like a mini-vacation, though seriously doubting she'd be able to do anything fun while she was there. After all, she was going to Texas to work, not play, and there'd be little time to fool around.

A tap at her door brought Kacey out of her thoughts. Swinging around, she waved Ariana into the room, noticing the bemused expression on her colleague's face.

"You really impressed Steve," Ariana informed Kacey, sliding into the chair near Kacey's desk.

"That's what I hoped to do," Kacey tossed back, returning to sit in front of her computer. "I've been working on this project for over a year, and I knew I'd only have one shot at getting him onboard."

"Oh, he's definitely behind you, honey. I've worked with Hadley for a long time and when he called Leon Archer personally from the conference room, I knew he was eager to move this project forward. He's sold. Don't think he's ever been as excited about a new line before."

"He's never seen swimsuits like mine before," Kacey countered with confidence.

"You're right about that," Ariana agreed, crossing her long legs and tilting back in her chair. She fluffed her bleached-white hair and puckered her full pink lips, a gesture that Kacey and her coworkers often mimicked when talking about Ariana. At fifty-six, Ariana Mendio was trim, shapely and still an alarmingly attractive woman. She'd been married three times; her current husband, Tony, was sixteen years her junior. He worked as a high-end menswear model for several fashion houses, a position that got Ariana and her boy-toy into exclusive society parties quite often. "SunKissed by Kacey is so sweet it could give a woman a toothache!" Ariana exclaimed with a giggle as she flicked her long fingers in the air toward Kacey.

Kacey laughed along with her coworker, shaking her head. "I don't plan to inflict any pain—only pleasure."

"I don't know. That black satin thong looked like it could put a hurting on some very tender spots."

"Please," Kacey shot back with a grin. "You know you're dying to wear it. In fact, I'm gonna send you the first manufacturer sample of that style as soon as it comes out of production. Size 8, right?" Kacey lifted a brow in question, her grin widening as she watched Ariana.

"Size 6, honey," Ariana corrected with a downward tilt of her head and a sweep of one hand over her flat stomach. "I've been hitting the gym with Tony."

"And it shows," Kacey finished, giving Ariana the compliment she'd been fishing for.

"Anyway, about SunKissed," Ariana went on. "I stopped by to tell you that Hadley wants me to get started on the marketing plan."

"Sounds good," Kacey replied.

"My thought is this. We position Leeman's as the first shopping stop that women must make before taking off on their next trip to the beach, to the pool or wherever the sun might take them. There's a swimsuit out there for every woman…"

"But finding the right one can take a whole lot of time," Kacey finished.

"Exactly. Shopping for swimwear can be a traumatic experience, but the eight styles offered through Sun-Kissed by Kacey make it a snap. I'm thinking our slogan could be 'Why Shop Anywhere Else?'"

"Why indeed?" Kacey agreed. "I love it! The bikinis, monokinis, full-coverage one-piece suits and two-piece styles offer multiple choices, especially since you can mix and match the bottoms and the tops."

A vigorous nod of assent from Ariana. "Your styles flatter all types of figures, and they're done in such luscious fabrics," she praised. "Archer Industries had better do a good job for us."

"For real. What do you know about the company?" Kacey asked, curious about where she was headed tomorrow and how she would get along with the owner.

"Only that it's a family-owned factory….employs most of the residents in Rockport. And in those parts… the Archer name has clout."

"Have you ever met Mr. Archer?"

Ariana shook her head. "No, but I've had more than a few conversations with him. He's a tough old bird who runs his factory with an iron fist. All about business. No warm fuzzies there."

"Gee, thanks for the warning," Kacey said, screwing up one side of her mouth. "Sounds like I'm in for a real test of wills—and skills."

"Well, don't worry too much," Ariana replied. "As long as you show up prepared to work long hours and take orders from a persnickety old man who really *can* run circles around his younger employees, you'll do fine."

"I'd better," Kacey murmured, beginning to feel the pressure of what she'd gotten herself into. Launching this line was a huge responsibility, and success depended on one thing: the perfect execution of her designs. Would Archer Industries deliver? Was she ready to place her future in the hands of a grumpy old man with no heart who couldn't possibly know what women want? *He may not know, but I do,* Kacey affirmed, determined to gain control of the process once she arrived in Rockport.

Chapter 3

Leon Archer Jr. drove his red Corvette convertible up the semicircular driveway that swept the front of his father's house and parked directly at the front door. Sitting back in his seat, he slid one hand over the smooth steering wheel and studied the black sedan already parked in the drive, the car that belonged to Gerald Ayers, his father's lawyer. What was going on? Why had his father summoned him to the house?

Leon had been a bit surprised when he arrived at the factory and had seen his father's parking spot empty. During all the years that Leon had worked at Archer Industries alongside his father, Leon Sr. had never failed to come to work by 6:00 a.m., making sure he arrived before his son or any of his employees reported for duty.

Now, curious about why his dad was still at home,

Leon turned his attention to the exterior of the hacienda-style mansion that his dad and mom had built nearly forty years ago. It had twenty rooms, seven bathrooms, an Olympic-size pool, a tennis court and a newly installed outdoor kitchen that rivaled anything shown on the home and garden shows that his mother loved to watch on television. The red tile roof sloped low over a center courtyard where exotic tropical flowers bloomed year-round. In fact, Leon Archer Sr.'s home had been featured in the prestigious *Southwest Homes* magazine, and continued to serve as the gathering spot for many Archer Industries company parties over the years. Since a good portion of Rockport residents either worked for Archer Industries or had a family member who did, most of the townsfolk had been hosted in the Archer home at one time or another.

Leon exited his car, slammed the door and strode up the flower-lined walkway. After letting himself in, Leon went directly to his father's study where the elder man was seated behind his walnut claw-foot desk, an unlit cigar stuck into the corner of his mouth. The sight made Leon smile…his mother had banned cigar smoking in the house long ago, but that didn't stop his old man from keeping up the appearance of enjoying a good smoke, especially when he was working at home.

"Hello, Dad. Hi, Gerald," Leon said as he greeted his father and the attorney who had handled Archer Industries' business for as long as Leon could remember. After a quick handshake with Gerald and a nod at his father, Leon sat down in the deep wingchair across from the huge, messy desk where Leon Sr. was busy signing papers that Gerald was handing to him.

"What's up? You doing okay?" Leon asked tentatively. Though his dad was seventy-four years old, and had never experienced any major health problems, Leon hoped his father's good luck had not taken an unexpected turn for the worse.

"Of course I'm okay," Leon Sr. shot back in a gruff voice, not looking up at his son. He placed another flourishing signature on a document and then muttered, "Why'd you ask something like that? Do I look sick to you?"

"No, no. Just wondering. When you didn't show up at the plant this morning, I got a little worried."

"No need," his father tossed out in a cavalier manner, now setting his pen aside. "I'm fine. In fact, I'm better than I've ever been, and God willing, I plan to stay that way for a long, long time."

"All right," Leon conceded, relieved by his father's bantering in his usually gruff voice. "So why are we here and not at work at the factory? There's a lot going on at the plant today. Three big orders came in last night and the Wilton shipment has to go out by noon."

"I know, I know," Leon Sr. acknowledged with a wave of one hand. "It'll all get done...don't worry. Nona's there, right?"

"Hey, you know she is. When I left yesterday, Nona was still on the phone arguing with FedEx over that package of samples from Seattle that got lost. I told her it could wait until today and for her to go home. She refused, so I left. Sometimes I think she takes her job way too seriously."

"Tell me about it," Leon Sr. agreed. He stopped what he was doing and pointed his cigar at his son. "She's a hard worker and great friend to all of us, but that woman needs a life. Other than her life at Archer, that is."

"Harrumph," Leon agreed with a shrug. "That's the truth."

"Well, you're the best person to handle her, I'm sure. She always does whatever you ask."

"Not always, but most of the time," Leon replied with a shake of his head, as if resigned to the fact that he had no choice but to tolerate the antics of his most trusted, but most temperamental, employee. "Okay... enough about Nona. What's really going on with you?" Leon wanted to know. He propped one foot on a knee and slipped back in his seat.

"Big changes," the elder Archer teased, raising his eyes from the final paper that the lawyer handed him to sign. He removed the unlit cigar from his mouth and set it aside. "This is what's up," he started, clasping his hands on his desk. "I'm retiring. As of this morning, I'm finished with the business."

Leon rolled his eyes in mock disbelief. "Oh? Really? And how many times have you said that?" he countered, knowing his father had made the same declaration several times before, only to renege on his decision and keep on working.

"I mean it this time," Leon Sr. said as he tapped his index finger on the stack of papers he'd signed and jerked his head toward his attorney. "Tell him, Gerald. It's done."

"That's right," the white-haired lawyer confirmed. "All the papers are in order. Your father has just made you the new owner of Archer Industries. It's all yours now."

Leon jerked forward, both hands steadied on his knees as he peered at his father in suspicion. "Is this for real?"

"Yes, for real. It's time for you to run the show, son, and I am more than ready to hand the whole thing over to you."

Leon sucked in a long breath and let the news settle in. He had known this day would come, but still, he was surprised. His father had made comments about retiring so many times that the running joke around the plant was that he'd leave when it snowed in Rockport, something that *had* happened, but nearly a century ago.

"Why now?" Leon wanted to know, wondering what had pushed his father to finally let go. He was an energetic man who walked four miles every day, ate only organic foods and never drank alcohol. And now that he'd given up cigars, his doctor had pronounced him healthier than ever.

"Because it's time."

"Are you telling me the truth?" Leon pressed. "You're not sick or anything, are you?"

"I'm in perfect health," his father replied with a snap. "In fact, that's the reason I'm doing this now. Your mother and I are leaving for a tour of Africa tomorrow. We're finally going on the trip we've put off for too many years. We decided last night that if we're going to go, we'd better go while I can still climb a mountain and stay up late enough to enjoy a sunset," Leon Sr. chuckled. "And we're taking our time, son. Probably be gone at least a month."

"A month, huh? Good for you!" But then Leon bit his bottom lip in concern. "Isn't this happening kinda fast?" He had thought he was prepared to take over the business, but now that Archer Industries had actually been turned over to him, the prospect of running things without his father nearby caught Leon off guard.

"Yes. That's right. No need to drag this out," Leon Sr. concurred. "It'll be an easy transition. I don't want any fancy retirement party or sappy farewells. I'm writing a personal letter to each employee, thanking them for their hard work and telling them they're in good hands. I know I can count on you to run the place the same way I have. So don't fuck things up, you hear?"

Leon had to laugh at his father's rare use of the F word.

"You practically grew up at the plant. You've been by my side since you were old enough to sit at my desk, so it won't take long for everyone to get used to taking orders from you instead of me."

"Orders?" Leon quipped. "I don't plan to run the place like a military operation."

His father laughed under his breath while brandishing his pen at his son. "Ha! That's what it takes to do business nowadays, son. The key is to act tough, keep everything under your control so no one gets the idea that they can operate outside the rules. If you're the man where the buck stops, then you're the man with the power…and you're gonna need power to succeed. You ready to be the boss?"

Leon hesitated, giving his mind a few seconds to wrap itself around the impact of his father's decision. The family company was now his to manage, and the responsibility was great. Was he prepared for the challenge and ready to step up to the plate?

"You bet I am," Leon confirmed with confidence, ready to make the difficult decisions that came with being in charge.

"I know you are, even though the old-timers will probably call you 'Junior,'" Leon's mother tossed out as she entered the room.

"Sara, that'll change now that he's the number one man," Mr. Archer told his wife, sending a scowl her way.

"I'll make sure of that," Leon agreed, warming to the idea that, at last, he'd be out from behind his father's shadow. Recently, he'd begun to feel confined, as if he were boxed into a place without an exit. Had his father sensed his restlessness? Was that what spurred his decision to retire? If so, the timing couldn't have been better.

Sara Archer, who stood a head shorter than her son, went over to him, patted him lightly on the cheek and reminded him in a sassy tone, "Well, you'll always be *Junior* to me."

Leon grimaced, and then broke into a smile, both annoyed and flattered by his mother's display of affection. As her only child, he had learned long ago that it did no good to protest her overprotective ways. As long as he lived, he would be her little boy and there was nothing he could do to change that.

"And I don't want you to worry about checking on the house while we're gone," Sara continued. "I gave Nona my keys so she can come in and water my plants and check on the aquarium. You'll have more important things on your mind than tending my African violets and feeding the fish."

"If that's what you and Nona arranged, it's fine with me," Leon conceded, aware of how much his mother liked and trusted Nona James, who was not only Archer

Industries' operations manager, but also a longtime family friend.

"I think that's it," Gerald Ayers stated as he snapped his briefcase closed and handed a packet of legal documents to the elder Archer, who put them into his safe.

Gerald leaned over to shake Leon's hand. "Congratulations, *Junior*," the lawyer said, beaming his approval.

Leon pumped the attorney's hand, "Thanks, Gerald."

"No problem. You're going to do fine." Turning to Leon Sr., the lawyer said, "If that's all you need from me, I'll be going. I've got to leave for the airport in an hour."

"Please don't tell me you're leaving the country, too," Leon remarked, concerned.

"No, not at all. Going to visit my daughter in Baton Rouge. I'm only a phone call away if you need me, Leon. Call anytime, and I'll be here…. Just as I've been for your father over the years."

"Whew! That's a relief," Leon said, knowing how much he was going to need the seasoned attorney's advice.

After Gerald left, Leon and his father reviewed the transition process, and then conducted an in-depth examination of the current production schedule.

"Next up is a women's swimsuit line for Leeman's," Leon Sr. informed his son.

"A swimsuit line, huh? That ought to be a pretty simple run. Steve Hadley's company out of New York, right?" Leon said, remembering the previous orders Hadley had placed with Archer Industries.

"Right. But this one might be a bit tricky. The designer wants to use a fabric that's gonna take some serious negotiating to get down to the price Hadley wants to pay. Some kind of a specialty blend they sourced out of China."

"Could be pricey," Leon said.

"Exactly what I thought, so I put our man in New Delhi on it. Hopefully, he'll find a better price in India," his father offered.

"Sounds good. Where do we stand on the Leeman's contract?" Leon asked.

"All done. I finalized everything with Steve Hadley. Here's the name of the rep from his store who is due here this afternoon to consult on the project," he said, handing Leon a piece of paper on which he had written the name. "Make sure everything comes off without a hitch, you hear? We can't afford to lose this account. We're doing fine, but profits were down a point last quarter."

"I know," Leon agreed, reading over the note, which read: Mr. Kacey Parker, Leeman's. "Don't worry. Leave all the business problems to me," Leon advised. "You and Mom go have fun in Africa."

"We plan to," his father replied. "But don't *you* have too much fun while we're gone, okay?"

Leon rolled his eyes in exaggeration. *How much fun could I possibly have if I'm busy turning triangles of exotic fabric into swimsuits for curvy females?* he wondered with a smile.

Chapter 4

The two-lane highway leading to Rockport, Texas, was bordered by flat coastal plains on one side and the surging Gulf of Mexico on the other. The black ribbon of asphalt stretching out before Kacey pulled her along, bringing her ever closer to her destination. Few cars passed hers on the highway, and most of the buildings she encountered were either low-slung ranch houses surrounded by acres of green pasture or weather-worn beach cottages raised high on stilts. Kacey had to admit that the sudden sense of isolation that hit her was eerily disturbing, yet peaceful.

Continuing northward, she shifted her gaze from the road to the sky, where not a single white cloud marred the huge expanse of blue that seemed to go on forever. This kind of openness, emptiness and lack of population was a definite contrast to what Kacey was used to.

An Easterner born and bred, she considered herself a typical urban working woman who thrived on deadlines, pressure and competition in a fast-paced environment that included long hours at the office, lots of take-out dinners and hitting the live entertainment circuit with her friends to relax. Leaving all that behind to hole up in this small town was going to require a great deal of patience, flexibility and trust.

When Kacey's cell phone rang, she checked the screen and saw that Linette was calling her back. Kacey answered, intending to keep it brief.

"Hey. Where are you?" she asked, knowing Linette was never in the same place for very long.

"At the airport. LAX," Linette sputtered, sounding out of breath. "Just got here, and wouldn't you guess… one of my bags is missing. This sucks. I'm shooting stills for Roberto Rogales's new outerwear campaign tomorrow and I need my equipment!"

"Right," Kacey replied, recalling the assignment Linette had accepted with the former Ralph Lauren protégé. "Glad that job worked out for you. But don't worry. Your bag will show. Happens all the time."

"It had better," Linette tossed back. "The schedule Roberto sent looks pretty scary and I've got a lot to do. Anyway, I got your message. What's up with you?"

"Well, right now I'm driving down a two-lane highway along the Texas Gulf Coast, on my way to the factory that is going to manufacture SunKissed by Kacey." She paused to let Linette absorb her good news. "Can you believe it?"

"Get outta here! For real? Hadley accepted your swimsuit line for Leeman's?"

"He did," Kacey confirmed with a smile, eagerly

filling Linette in on the details of her meeting with her boss and her upcoming stay in Rockport.

"That's sooo exciting," Linette said, clearly happy for Kacey. "Your swimsuits are the bomb! They're gonna be a huge hit. I've never seen any like them."

"Your photos played a big part in winning Hadley over. And once the manufacturer's samples are finished, I want you to shoot those, too. My plan is to convince Hadley to send our models to Rockport for the fittings and the promotional photos. Think you can squeeze in a trip to Texas when I get to that point?"

"Of course. Count on it," Linette assured Kacey. "I should wrap up this job by the end of the week. Just give me a call and I'll be there."

"Great. By the time the samples are ready to be photographed, I'll be more than ready for some company. This temporary exile to Texas is not what I expected to be doing right now."

"Hey, I hear you. Just focus on your work and time will fly by," Linette advised in a rushed voice. "Hey, gotta go. My bag is here! We'll talk later, okay?"

"Right," Kacey agreed, ending the call and already missing her friend.

While Linette was rubbing shoulders with Hollywood types in Los Angeles, Kacey would be stuck with an old man in a factory in Texas. *But it'll be worth it,* she reminded herself, refocusing on the road, surprised to see that a herd of black and white cows had gathered along the barbed-wire fence running parallel to the highway, their large brown eyes trained on her. Shaking her head in disbelief, she turned up the volume on the CD player and let Whitney's new album fill the car.

Half an hour after leaving the Corpus Christi airport,

Kacey finally came to a billboard splashed with large red and blue letters that announced, *Welcome to Rockport. Home of Archer Industries.* Slowing down, she leaned over and scrutinized the huge sign, which showcased a two-story industrial building constructed of dark red brick, flanked by groves of leafy palm trees. A mature man was posed in front of the structure, chin raised high, a big smile on his face, his deep brown skin burnished like polished wood. In his dark business suit with his arms crossed at his chest he exuded the aura of a successful businessman.

"Old man Archer," Kacey decided, thinking the older man looked pleasant enough. Maybe working with him wouldn't be so bad after all.

Driving on, Kacey arrived at the center of town where a gas station, a convenience store, a beauty shop and a hardware outlet anchored the four corners of the old-fashioned square. Beyond the hub of the town, Kacey caught glimpses of lacey Victorian homes on broad green lawns, as well as modest bungalow-type homes facing each other across grassy esplanades. The quaint scene that greeted her was picturesque, charming and serene. Pretty to look at but not a place where she wanted to spend any more time than was absolutely necessary.

"I'd be bored out of my skull if I had to live here," Kacey murmured as she inched along the town's main street, where a scattering of people were busy running errands or chatting in clusters on the wide cement sidewalks.

At the far end of the main street, she saw Seaside Suites, the economy motel where she'd booked a room for the duration. The exterior of the nondescript building was in desperate need of a paint job and there were only three other cars in the parking lot, which adjoined a run-down apartment complex surrounded by a chain-link fence.

I'll check in after I meet with Mr. Archer, Kacey decided, glad she'd worn her Donna Karan navy suit and comfortable heels on the plane, so she could go straight to her meeting. She checked her makeup in the rearview mirror, pressed her shapely burgundy-tinted lips together and fluffed her honey-brown curls with one hand. Satisfied that all was fine, she nodded at her image. After all, she was representing Leeman's, one of the most exclusive retailers in the country. A good first impression was essential, and she planned to let Mr. Archer know from the get-go that she was not some underling who was there to take orders from him, but a designer whose swimsuit line was going to become the hottest fashion label in swimwear.

Slowly passing the motel, Kacey eyed the drab appearance of her future home and sighed. The thought of living there made her heart sink, but she refused to let it get her down.

"Oh, well, at least it's not raining," Kacey remarked, resigned to toughing it out for as long as it took to finish the job she'd come to do.

The woman who met Kacey in the lobby of the Archer Industries building greeted her with a vise grip of a handshake and a hearty hello.

"Welcome to Archer Industries. I'm Nona James. Operations manager," she said in a flat Texas accent that seemed to solidify her connection to the small-town plant.

"Hello, Nona. Kacey Parker. Good to meet you," Kacey said, eyeing the woman closely. She was at least a head taller than Kacey—big-boned, buxom and very statuesque. The makeup on her buff-hued face was flawless, but a bit heavy-handed, as were the intricate chandelier earrings dangling from her ears. An African-print headband held an explosion of natural hair off her face, creating a dark halo of frizz that translated into an inspired resemblance of a young Diana Ross.

"I'm so glad you're here," Nona said, her red lips widening into a full-blown grin. "Did you check into the motel? I assume you're staying at the Seaside. It's the best we have around here."

"I drove past on my way through town. It looks fine. I'll check in after I finish here," Kacey replied, taking care not to imply that the accommodations might not be up to snuff.

"Okay. If you need anything, let me know. The manager of the Seaside is my cousin, so I'll be on his case if you have any complaints."

"Sounds great. I'm anxious to get settled and started on production," Kacey replied, glancing around the sun-splashed lobby where large Lucite boxes showcased some of the clothes produced by Archer Industries. On display were activewear, all-weather jackets, chlorine-resistant swimsuits and water aerobic wear, which included pool shoes, sun hats and beach towels.

"Mr. Archer isn't here at the moment, but he's on his way in," Nona said. "He's eager to meet you. Come on back. You can wait in his office," Nona said, leading Kacey down a carpeted hallway toward a cluster of offices at the back of the building. "Can I get you something to drink?" she asked after escorting Kacey into a very spacious room where an oval conference table took up a good portion of the space. The table was crowded with papers, fabric samples, pattern books and cutting tools. Clearly, this was more of a workroom than an executive suite.

"Some cold water would be great," Kacey replied, before settling into a gray suede chair.

"No problem. Be right back," Nona said as she left the room.

Left alone, Kacey looked around, curious to learn what she could about Mr. Archer before he showed up. Groupings of framed certificates, awards and permits hung on the wall behind his desk. One family photo caught her attention. It was of a much younger Mr. Archer, seated on a sofa with an attractive woman whom Kacey guessed was his wife. On her lap sat a young boy holding a puppy, grinning into the camera.

He's a family man, Kacey mused, beginning to feel more comfortable about working with the man who had promised Steve Hadley that he could turn her dreams into reality.

"One bottle of cold water, right?"

The deep tenor voice forced Kacey's eyes from the photo. She turned toward the door and quickly saw that the person at the entryway was definitely not Nona James, but a drop-dead gorgeous man who was grinning at her as if pleasantly surprised to find her sitting in Mr. Archer's office. The man slanted his slender body against the doorframe and proceeded to trace a less than businesslike gaze over Kacey, emitting bold signals of more than a casual interest in her.

Since he seemed in no hurry to speak, Kacey countered by taking her time inspecting the guy. He had jet-black hair with a hint of waviness, cut close with a razor part. The angular planes of his face accented his vibrant pecan-brown skin and made his intriguing gray eyes impossible to ignore. His light blue oxford shirt was open at the collar. His crisply creased tan khaki pants were held in place by a beautiful leather belt that Kacey immediately recognized as one of Cole Haan's most popular designs, and the soft Italian leather shoes on his feet matched his ultraexpensive belt.

Not bad, Kacey decided, pleased to find such a put-together, preppy-looking brother in the middle of nowhere. He was attractive, in a sexy, clean-cut way, sending out signals of a conservative dresser who certainly had good taste.

"Oh. The water. Yes. Thanks," Kacey replied in a breathy voice that sounded as if it were coming from someone else. She stood, accepted the bottle of water and waited for him to speak, wondering what department this brother worked in at Archer and if she would be lucky enough to work with him.

The man stepped fully into the room. "So I can see that you're not *Mr.* Parker?"

Kacey laughed, watching as he analyzed her reaction. "Oh, yes, but it's *Ms.* Kacey Parker."

"Well, I have to admit, I wasn't expecting…" he stuttered, pulling out the piece of paper his father had handed him. "I guess…"

"You assumed I was a man?" Kacey finished with a hint of a challenge.

He gave her a sheepish smile and nodded. "Yeah. Guess we all did."

"Happens all the time," she concluded, shaking the

man's hand. "Hope you're not too disappointed," she finished.

"Not at all," he replied with appreciative emphasis. "I'm Leon Archer. Good to meet you." Then he walked around the desk, keeping his eyes riveted on Kacey as he eased into the chair, clearly as if he belonged there.

Kacey slipped back into her seat, crossed her legs as well as her arms, and blinked, confused. *"You're* Mr. Archer?" she started, fishing for an explanation.

"Right. I'm Leon Archer." A beat, and then he added with a heart-pounding grin, "Junior."

"Ahh…then you must be Mr. Archer's…"

"Son," Leon finished. "As well as the new owner of Archer Industries," he clarified his statement with a downward tilt of his head. Looking up at Kacey, he said, "As of this morning, in fact."

"Oh, well…" she stammered. "Really? Then I guess congratulations are in order," she offered, sensing a definite increase in her pulse. So, the grumpy old man was out, and his superfine son was in? How'd she get so lucky? All of her worry about having to work with a crotchety old man had been wasted. Now, she had to worry about keeping her composure while his son's metal-gray eyes devoured her!

"Thanks," Leon said in a pride-filled manner. He propped his left elbow on the desk to rest his chin on curled fingers, which Kacey noted bore no rings.

"When did this change of leadership happen? I was prepared to meet with your father," Kacey stated, feeling her professional façade begin to melt under Leon Jr.'s disturbing stare. He certainly wasn't trying to hide his personal interest in her, and Kacey was definitely feeling flattered.

Breaking his gaze at last, Leon grinned. "Happened this morning. Dad unexpectedly decided to step down to enjoy his golden years traveling with my mom. They're leaving for Africa tomorrow."

"Oh, so soon?"

"Yeah. But don't worry about your swimsuits. You're in good hands."

"I'm sure I am," Kacey murmured, sensing a wave of heat surge through her stomach and ease down between her thighs, initiating a hint of dampness in her panties. *Get a grip, girl,* she silently admonished, forcing back a smile. "So *you'll* be working with me on production, then?" she had to clarify.

"Absolutely," Leon confirmed in a much bigger voice. "I'm totally familiar with the project, so you're stuck with me. Unless you'd prefer to work with Nona, my operations manager. She's been here almost as long as I have and can handle every stage of the process."

"No, that's all right," Kacey offered, a tad too quickly. Composing herself, she folded her hands together. "If you're on top of everything and can deliver what I want, that's all that counts."

"Trust me. I can deliver *whatever* you want. Just let me know what it is," he assured, using a voice that was so intentionally sexy that Kacey shivered, unable to think of a comeback.

This man is such a flirt, she decided, aware that he was no longer smiling. In fact, his hooded eyes were now slits of challenge, as if daring her to make him prove that he could deliver on more fronts than the production line.

"I'll definitely let you know," she tossed back with a lift of one shoulder, prepared to play his game of words.

"But I'm warning you, I can be very demanding, and particular."

"So can I," he replied with a hint of mockery.

"Fine. I'd love to see how we operate together."

"I was thinking the same thing. I have no doubt we're gonna get along just fine." The room fell quiet as Leon opened a folder and removed the photos that Hadley had emailed to the manufacturer. "I love your line. The designs are stunning. Utterly unique."

"Thanks," Kacey replied.

"You really know how to showcase a woman's best assets."

"That's what good design is all about," she replied, watching Leon as he held up one of the photos and tilted back in his chair.

"I especially love this one...your Sheer Double Dip," he commented, moving the picture aside to rake Kacey with a look that left no doubt in her mind that he was checking out more than her design credentials.

"It's the heart of my collection. All about the see-through fabric. Do you have a supplier for it, yet?"

"We're sourcing it now. Trust me, I'll get it at your price."

"Good. Then I guess we've got a lot to do," Kacey tossed out, clearly ready to get started.

"Sounds fine. I'm ready whenever you are," Leon said, leaning forward.

Kacey slowly unscrewed the cap on her bottle of water while assessing her new collaborator with interest. Though caught off guard by this shift in plans, the prospect of working with Leon Archer Jr. absolutely intrigued her. In the full five minutes since they'd met, she could already tell that collaborating with him was going to be a challenge. A challenge that she was more than ready to accept.

Chapter 5

Over the next hour, Kacey and Leon discussed each design in detail and shared thoughts on the execution of the various styles. They collaborated on pattern adjustments that would simplify production and keep costs down. However, it became clear right away that even though they shared the common goal of turning out a dynamite product at the best possible price, Leon was much more relaxed about the time frame than Kacey was.

"When will the first samples be ready?" she wanted to know.

"Depends," he casually replied.

"On what?"

"On how fast Bob Truett can get to your project."

"Bob Truett?" Kacey questioned.

"Our master patternmaker. He's the person who really

holds the power around here," Leon chuckled. "He's the best, though. Been with the company for years."

"You know I want to move this along as quickly as possible, don't you?" Kacey reminded Leon, not wanting to waste a second.

"We don't rush things around here. We move at the best pace to get the job done right, on schedule and to the customer's satisfaction."

"I'm sure you do, but I can't stick around Rockport forever."

"Don't be in such a rush. Relax. The workroom is pretty busy right now, but Truett knows your contract is a quick turnaround job," he assured Kacey, examining a page from the folder that contained the production schedule for SunKissed. "If all goes well, we should have your samples completed within a few days. However, I don't like to ask my employees to work overtime unless it's absolutely necessary."

Kacey simply watched Leon and held back from speaking while he scanned the document in silence. When he glanced up, he hooked Kacey with his magnetic gray eyes once again, creating an electric connection that made Kacey's heart turn over. Gulping back her unsettling reaction, she stilled, determined not to expose the stir of emotions cascading through her body.

"But you will ask for overtime if you have to, right?" she finally asked.

"Let's just see how things go," was all Leon offered.

"All right," Kacey conceded, hoping he would not be reluctant to push his employees hard to get the job done in record time. But that was his call to make, not hers, so she'd just have to trust him to do what he felt was best.

As he continued to explain the process, Kacey's eyes settled on Leon's full, well-formed lips, unable to keep from fantasizing about the warm, yummy taste she knew they would leave on her tongue. The idea of kissing Leon Archer made her nipples go hard in her bra and the core of her womanhood tense up. Such an intensely sexual arousal, prompted by a man she did not know, was like a lightning strike on a sunny day—completely out of the blue, but not impossible. In fact, getting excited over a man she did not know was exactly what she'd been yearning to feel for a very long time.

Kacey's personal life hummed along in an easy, uncomplicated way that she'd come to consider as normal. She didn't have a special man in her life, but she did have Jamal, the guy she turned to whenever she needed someone to rescue her from long spells of sexual abstinence. Kacey trusted and loved Jamal as a true friend, even though he wished she could love him like a man.

Jamal. Thinking of him made Kacey almost sigh. They'd known each other for eight years, and as much as she tried to shift her feelings for the devilishly handsome real estate investor into full romantic mode, it never quite happened. So, she'd settled on remaining good friends with occasional benefits, a perfect arrangement for Kacey, despite Jamal's desire for more.

When Leon cleared his throat with a fist to his mouth, as if aware of how distracted Kacey had become, she snapped to attention. Taking in his bemused expression, she tossed her crazy imaginings aside, placing fingertips to her chin to feel grounded in the moment.

"Ready to discuss the schedule?" Leon started, lifting one eyebrow while gracing her with a look as intimate as a kiss, which only served to rev her pulse a notch higher.

He's as caught up as I am, Kacey observed, exchanging a slow smile with him. "Sure," she replied, squeezing her legs together in an attempt to banish the itch that was definitely in need of scratching. Leaning forward in her chair, she focused her attention on the papers spread out on Leon's desk, avoiding his eyes completely.

"First, let's talk about your fabric," he stated.

"What do you think about the choices?" she asked Leon, her voice now crisply professional and efficient.

"Very nice. We have everything in stock except the imported Naughty Net, but we ought to find it soon."

"Perfect," Kacey commented. "And I'd like to come in at least five percent under budget," she told him, plunging back to earth with a definite crash, determined to make good on her promise to Hadley.

"Five percent? I dunno," Leon hedged. "You have eight different styles, and each one requires a lot of decorative detail. The cost of your raw materials eats up more than one-third of your budget," Leon warned with a tone of authority. "You might want to consider eliminating some of the expensive bling if you want to cut costs."

His candid assessment quickly dissolved Kacey's dreamy reaction to him. He sounded way too confident that she would be willing to go along with whatever he decided. Well, she had news for Leon Archer. His flirtatious overtures weren't going to distract her from holding firm on her designs. She knew her swimsuits contained the flashy touches that made them stand out from all the other swimwear currently available, and she had no plans to change that.

Certainly, this guy didn't expect her to drop the metallic gold rings on her bikini tops, did he? Or omit the polished Italian stone side clasps on the bottoms? Or trash the bronze beading on halter ties shot through with strands of gold and silver thread?

No, she could never eliminate her trademark sparkle or dull the shine that she adored.

"I have to disagree with your assessment," she told Leon firmly, after taking her time considering his point. "The accessory trim is what *makes* my styles, along with the custom cuts and imported fabrics. Unique accessorizing is key."

"I understand. But that's where the financial wiggle room is," Leon advised.

Kacey inclined her head in agreement, thinking about the financial bonus that Hadley had promised if she reduced production costs. Somehow, she had to prove to Hadley that she could get the job done, and done at his price.

"I understand where you're coming from, Leon," she finally agreed. "However, we'll have to cut costs someplace else."

Leon simply lifted his palms toward the ceiling as if at a loss to suggest an alternative.

"The estimates for labor per unit and packaging look good," Kacey said, searching for a way to make it all work.

"Oh, yes. Those are static costs that remain as is. No wiggle room there," Leon confirmed.

"Okaaay…so, if accessory trim is the wild card,"

Kacey restated, turning her thoughts to ways of saving money without sacrificing style, "I have an idea."

"Let's hear it," Leon prompted.

Kacey sank back in her chair, fingers tented at her lips, knowing she would have to adjust costs somewhere if she wanted that bonus money. Leaning forward, she launched her suggestion. "What if, instead of *eliminating* the more expensive trim, we simply reduce the quantity?"

"You know, that was going to be my next suggestion," Leon replied, appearing excited by her approach. He flipped through Kacey's portfolio and tapped a page with his finger. "Like the Lucite squares on this Retro Hipster style. The halter top has Lucite squares on the ends of the ties, and two smaller pieces at the bustline. Maybe if we use one larger piece, you'd get the same effect and spend less on trim."

Kacey made a subtle nod, knowing his solution made sense. Eliminating one piece of Lucite detail wouldn't detract from the overall look, and if this was what she had to do to make this line happen, she was willing to give it a try.

"Okay," she agreed with Leon, her earlier irritation beginning to ease. "I'll review each style and see where I can make similar adjustments."

"Great," Leon replied, pausing to review the last page of the production schedule before he spoke again. "Once you've done that, I'll revise the manufacturing estimate and email it to you so that you can send it over to Hadley for his approval."

"Fantastic," Kacey replied, ready to tackle the numbers, and pleased that Leon was onboard. The more energy he focused on her swimsuit line, the more quickly she'd be able to return to New York, even though her earlier determination to get out of Rockport as fast as she could didn't seem quite so pressing anymore.

"One thing I guess you've learned about me," Leon said after their revision session wound down. "I'm committed one hundred percent to making sure you *are* happy."

"What more could I ask for?" Kacey replied, buzzed by the sense of partnership that was rapidly developing between them. On this project, which was so special for Kacey, working with a talented African-American man who had the power, the insight and the creative drive to deliver on her vision was a drastic, and wonderful, development.

While doing promotional work for Leeman's, her vision and taste had been challenged many times. However, to stay on track and not become distracted by exaggerated promises from suppliers and vendors, she'd adopted a three-point approach that worked for her: Always be clear and upfront about her expectations, never sacrifice quality for quantity and steer clear of obvious over-the-top trends with limited appeal. Now she had to add one more point to her list: Never fantasize about making love with the manufacturer!

Finished with their meeting, Leon stood and motioned for Kacey to come with him. "I've set up a workspace for you to use while you're here. It's not very big, I'm afraid," he said, leading her down the hall to a small cubicle not far from his office. It was private, quiet and had a phone, a computer and a drafting table. All the equipment she needed to do her job.

Kacey followed him into the space, very aware of his

closeness, his scent and especially the silent electricity crackling in the air. His presence sucked her in, tingled her imagination and made her want to do things she hadn't thought of before. Like make the first move and kiss the hell out of this guy who was pushing her most intimate buttons.

"And you do have a window," Leon offered with a wave of one hand, moving to open the blinds and reveal a clear view of the parking lot.

Kacey moved toward the window, her shoulder brushing Leon's as she stepped past him, certain she'd felt him tense when their bodies touched. "That's the road that leads to the Coast, isn't it?" she asked, recognizing the highway that she'd taken on her way to Rockport.

"Right. If you hang a left out of the parking lot and go four miles, you'll hit Aransas Bay." He moved up behind her, so near that his breath warmed her neck and sent delightful shivers down Kacey's spine. "I live out that way, too. On the beach."

"You do?" she commented, turning around, her face stopping only inches from his, so near their lips could have easily met. And held. In a long, delicious kiss. The subtle sensuousness that shimmered between them was like an invisible thread, drawing them together. Neither took a backward step, yet a message of caution flashed into Kacey's brain, warning her to move—steer clear of temptation and concentrate on something other than his arresting grin, which was rattling her composure and provoking a ruffle of a smile on her lips. "Must be nice, living near the water," she said, her voice breathy and low. She enunciated her words slowly, as if carefully calibrating her reply to lead him into more personal revelations.

"It is nice," he agreed. "It's quiet out on the beach. Very private. I live alone, so it's a welcome escape from all the noise and hectic hours I put in here at the factory."

He lives alone, Kacey quickly registered, certain he'd deliberately dropped that nugget of private information to disarm any resistance she might have had about entering into a more intimate level of conversation. Deciding to play the game she knew he'd started, she lobbed the comeback she hoped he was expecting. "I hear you. My job at Leeman's can get pretty crazy, too, so going home to a quiet place…with no one around, is heaven."

"Do you live in Manhattan?" Leon quickly probed.

"No, in Harlem. But I'm planning on moving into the city when I return."

"I'll bet it's expensive, living in New York. Any roommates?"

"No, just me."

"So you like big-city life?"

"I love it. Born and raised in Harlem. Wouldn't give up New York for anything."

"Well, it's all about how you want to live your life," he replied laughingly, now stepping back to put more space between them. "Small town Texas is where I come from and Rockport has always been home. It's really a great place to live and work."

"Especially if you're an Archer, I'll bet," Kacey finished with a chuckle.

"Oh, yeah," he sheepishly acknowledged. "Guess you got me there."

With a duck of her head Kacey stepped even further away from Leon and put both of her hands on the back of the stool in front of her drafting table. Holding on to it, she watched Leon carefully, her heart racing in her chest. If he didn't leave soon, she knew she might embarrass herself by revealing more than she should, or asking too many questions. But she wasn't going to be in Rockport for long, and time would fly by. Would there be enough time to get to know Leon Archer better? And why did she feel so compelled to get answers to the questions that were crowding her mind?

"Think I'd better get busy on those revisions," she told him, slipping onto the stool. She picked up a pencil and pointed it at him. "I'll let you know when I'm finished."

"Good idea. Just push the red button on your phone and that'll buzz me in my office. When you're ready, I'd like to show you around the plant."

"Will do," Kacey replied. As she watched Leon leave her cubicle, she couldn't resist a shake of her head. Whew! That man was yanking all her chains and she didn't plan to stop him.

Chapter 6

Once Kacey had reviewed the revised production budget, she sent it to Steve Hadley, proud of herself, and Leon, for accomplishing their mission. Within fifteen minutes, Hadley replied to her email, congratulating her on reducing overall costs by seven percent and assuring her that he'd work out a contractor's agreement for her and that she would receive a nice bonus once the product had been received. Pleased with her achievement, as well as her boss's reply, she buzzed Leon, who quickly returned to her cubicle.

"Now that money matters are settled, let's take a tour of the factory," Leon suggested, lingering in the entry.

Kacey smiled, allowing herself to relax and savor the importance of the moment. Everything was falling into place. The tension that had been building inside her since launching her proposal for Hadley in New York began to dissipate. Partnering with Leon was going to be a definite change from anything she'd ever done, and she hoped there'd be no bumps in the road. But with his steel-gray eyes all over her and the hint of his cologne filling her head, it was going to be awfully damn hard to concentrate on work.

But I have to, she reminded herself, biting her lip as she powered down her computer. She shouldn't even be conjuring up romantic notions about a man she hardly knew. It was time to get serious about the work she'd come here to do.

"You guys about finished?"

Glancing up, Kacey saw that Nona had come up behind Leon and placed a ring-laden hand on his shoulder. When Nona's fingers grazed her boss's neck, Kacey squinted in surprise, thinking that was a pretty intimate gesture for an operations manager to make with the man who owned the place. However, Leon didn't seem bothered at all.

"Yeah. I'm about to give Kacey a tour of the plant," Leon replied, shifting more fully into Kacey's cubicle and away from Nona's touch.

Nona, who was holding a thick black binder in her other hand, followed him into the room. "Leon, I know you have a ton of things to take care of…with Mr. Archer leaving so sudden and all. Want me to show Kacey around, introduce her to the key people who'll be involved in the production?"

Leon tapped a finger on the corner of Kacey's desk as if considering Nona's suggestion. "No, that's okay. I'll show Kacey around."

"All right," Nona replied, sounding a tad disappointed. She smiled at Kacey and shrugged. "Guess I'll see you later." Then she left the room in a swish of African print fabric.

Turning to Kacey, Leon said, "Come on. Let's go out on the floor and get acquainted with everyone. We've got a lot to cover today."

Seated at her desk, Nona tossed back her head, jutted out her bottom lip and glared at the ceiling. With her eyes squinted into long-lashed slits, she pressed her tongue to the roof of her mouth. The swimsuit designer was much too attractive for Nona's liking. A slick, sexy professional woman from New York City could become a real distraction.

If Kacey Parker thinks Leon is gonna spend all his time fawning over her, she's sadly mistaken. But at least she won't be here that long, Nona decided, feeling a sweep of relief as she picked up a folder and got into her work for the day.

Kacey and Leon entered the corridor leading to the heart of the plant, walking side by side while making small talk about the factory.

"We pride ourselves on turning out high-quality items at competitive pricing levels," Leon told Kacey as he touted his company's track record with pride. "Our design capability and fabric quality is competitive with any name brand. Our motto, 'We Suit Every Body' is more than a catchy slogan. We mean it!"

"How long has your family been in business?" Kacey wanted to know.

"Fifty-two years."

"And you've been working here since…?"

"Since forever, it seems. My dad made me start out

at the bottom to learn the business from the ground up. My first real job was on the packing line…part-time while I was in high school," Leon replied, in a voice laden with pride. "Worked right alongside Nona, who started here the same day."

"Oh, really? She's been here that long?"

"Oh, yeah. Most of my classmates worked here at one time or another. Especially during summer vacations. We worked hard, but goofed off a lot, too. As soon as we'd get off work, we used to head straight to the beach and go skinny dipping. We'd stay out on the beach all night sometimes."

"You all swam in the nude?" Kacey had to comment, imagining how fine Leon must have looked when he was younger, and buck naked. Not that he wasn't fine now, because it was clear he took good care of himself.

The smothered laughter that bubbled up from Leon's throat was the only answer Kacey needed. "Sure. Why not?" he said. "We were young…friends just having fun. Nobody bothered us." A beat. "Our favorite place to swim was Barker's Bend. Wow, it's been a long time since I've thought about that." Shaking his head, Leon turned into another hallway and escorted Kacey through a set of metal double doors.

Kacey increased her pace to keep up with Leon, whose long strides were moving them along quickly. Anxious to keep him talking, she threw out the question she was burning to have answered. "So you and Nona have been friends a long time, huh?"

"Yeah. I've known her about all my life."

"So you two are…close?" she prompted, unable to shake the image of Nona's hand placed so possessively on Leon's shoulder and his apparent lack of displeasure.

One question was burning in her mind: *Did you two have a romantic relationship? What does she mean to you now?* But of course she couldn't ask that.

"Close? Oh, sure," Leon blithely confirmed with a flick of his hand. "My mom was her mother's best friend. When Nona's mother died, my mom kinda adopted Nona, so she's like a member of my family, really."

"I see," Kacey murmured. But that didn't explain the obvious possessiveness that Kacey had detected in Nona's attitude. Something told Kacey that she'd better watch Nona James closely and try not to get on her bad side.

Inside the noisy heart of the factory, Leon paused to let Kacey take in the buzz of activity swirling around them. Here industrial sewing machines and power-cutting tools were actively turning fabric into a variety of products. As they toured the plant, Leon pointed out the various stages of production as articles of clothing passed from cutting tables to sewing machines, pressing equipment and the final staging area for inventory storage and shipping.

"This is where everything happens," he explained. "Workers in that section on the left complete the manual steps needed to prepare the product before the tools and machines take over. Each employee has a specific job to do, and timing is critical…not only to maintain a steady production flow, but also to ensure a safe environment. If one person drops the ball, it can affect the entire run, so team effort is vitally important."

"That kind of interdependence probably helps create the family-type vibe that I can definitely feel around here," Kacey commented as she slid her gaze over the massive machinery where men and women were busy with their work.

Leon beamed his pleasure at Kacey's spot-on observation. "Absolutely right. We work hard together, we live close to each other and we depend on one another to get the job done right."

"That must be a good feeling…knowing your coworkers so well."

"Yes, it's a definite benefit of living in a small town where no one is a stranger."

"No one?" Kacey repeated, beginning to feel less like an intruder.

He turned back to Kacey, his face soft and somber. "No one," he repeated in a husky voice that delivered the seriousness of his message. "Not even you." He placed a hand on her arm, his fingers lingering on the sleeve of her navy jacket. "I mean that, Kacey. While you're here, I plan to do all I can to make you feel like a part of the Archer family."

The raw sensuousness in his voice sent involuntary shivers of arousal through Kacey, who lifted her face to Leon's. He'd said "the Archer family," hadn't he? Not the "Archer Industries family," making Kacey wonder if Leon was aware of the slip of the tongue he'd made.

"Thanks. I'd like that," she murmured, impressed by his genuine effort to put her at ease.

The tender expression that suffused his features told her that she'd interpreted his comment exactly as he'd hoped. "I want your experience here to be well worth your time," he went on, leading her deeper into the workroom.

He stopped at a metal rail that separated the walkway

from the work area, removed his hand from her arm and dipped his head. "I know Rockport is nothing like New York, but I think my hometown is a pretty special place. We have a lot to offer." The clacking cacophony of sounds that reverberated through the factory forced Leon to step closer to Kacey so that she could hear what he had to say. Continuing in a much stronger voice, he told her, "Since you're going to be around for a while, I hope you'll take the time to get to know the city…and me…a lot better."

"I hope so, too," Kacey confessed, aware of the vibrations from the massive machinery that suddenly engulfed them. Or was it the hum of her fast-racing heart that was causing the steady pulsations rocketing through her body?

Kacey gave Leon an affirmative nod, turned around and started down the walkway. He riveted his eyes on her exquisite backside, swallowing the lump of appreciation that crowded his throat. With her head held high, she sashayed to the end of the catwalk, and into a section that was walled off by a large section of glass. Leon followed close behind.

"I want you to meet Bob Truett, the head patternmaker I told you about," Leon said to Kacey as he guided her over to the man behind the glass wall who was busy moving pattern pieces around on his computer screen. "Bob Truett," Leon started, "this is Kacey Parker. The designer for the SunKissed line."

Bob, a short stocky man with a receding hairline who resembled Danny DeVito, shifted in his seat, looked up and beamed a toothy smile at Kacey. "Welcome to Archer," he said. "I was just uploading some of your specs."

"Great to meet you," Kacey replied, moving closer to his computer screen to study the images floating there, relieved to see that he was using the same CAD software that she used in New York. By storing her design styles and color choices on disks, they were easily accessed and managed. "Looks good," she commented perusing his work.

"Bob's a real whiz at pulling off computerized replicas of the most complicated clothing constructions," Leon agreed.

"Mind if I watch for a while?" Kacey asked.

"No, not at all," Bob replied, waving her into the empty chair beside his. "In fact, I need your input. Oh, and we'll receive the Naughty Net from India day after tomorrow."

"Fantastic," Kacey said, relieved to know that Archer had come through.

"Something I need to know now," Truett started. "Do you want the shirring on this tie-side bottom to run all the way around the hipline or just across the front?"

Scooting closer to the screen, Kacey studied the image and launched into her vision of the style, while Bob made the necessary adjustments in the pattern.

Leon retreated to the back of Bob's workstation to observe. *Damn, that woman is pretty!* he thought, pulling in a long, silent breath. *And talented, too,* he acknowledged. Kacey, the fashion designer, was the artistic force behind the line, and he was proud to act as the vehicle to channel her finished products into the heart of the apparel industry. Together, they could make a heck of a pair.

Was that why he was drawn to her like a magnet picking up pins from the cutting-room floor? Why the attraction he'd felt when he first saw her sitting in his office had hit him like a jolt of fresh air? He was still reeling from the encounter. When he'd discussed the Leeman's contract with his father, he had assumed he'd be working with some flighty male artistic type from New York, never expecting to be paired with a sexy woman who had so much going on. What a lucky break! And she'd told him that she lived alone, so she must be single. No roommates. No rings. No mention of a kid or a significant other she'd left behind in New York. He sure hoped Kacey Parker was as special, and available, as she appeared to be because he was going to do all he could to keep her in Rockport as long as possible.

As he listened to Kacey and Bob discussing the various stages that her samples would go through, Leon was impressed anew by the unusual creative flair of her swimwear. She certainly knew how to capitalize on a woman's best features while softening the appearance of those ever-present flaws. He'd never seen any female on the beach in a suit close to what SunKissed by Kacey had to offer, and he could hardly wait to see the finished products.

"What size do you want the samples made in?" Truett asked, busily re-creating the extra-wide straps of a white halter top on his computerized patternmaker.

"I think it might be best…" Kacey began, but was cut off when Leon's voice drifted from behind her and interrupted her reply.

"Bob, I think you should make the samples in Ms. Parker's size. Whatever that is," he finished, deliberately inserting a hint of a taunt in his comment.

Kacey's head whipped around and she glared at Leon, who simply let a sly smile curve his lips.

"For your information I wear a size 4...petite," she informed him without hesitation, clearly ready to accept his challenge.

So, she's game, Leon thought, his heart thudding at the thought of her wearing the sexy swimsuits now floating across Bob's computer monitor.

"If I were in New York," Kacey continued, "I'd have the in-house models at Leeman's fit them. I even considered having the models come to Rockport for the shoot, but I've changed my mind completely. Since I'm on a tight deadline and don't have time to ship the samples back to New York, I may as well fit them myself."

"Good point," Bob acknowledged, punching in more numbers. "That way I can make the adjustments on the spot and save a lot of time."

"Great," Kacey stated. "I can't wait until the samples are ready."

Neither can I, Leon silently admitted, realizing his suggestion hadn't thrown Kacey at all.

"If you're going to test-model the swimsuits, then Nona can help you with the fittings," Truett told Kacey.

Sorry, Bob, Leon quietly mused. *That'll be one job that belongs to the boss, even though Kacey doesn't know it...yet.*

Leon crossed the space between himself and Kacey to add a comment on one of her designs. "I like this black one-piece style. It's the definition of classic! It's sexy, and yet it's not like those teeny-weeny string silhouettes that show off a lot of skin. Your suits have glamour and class. Like old-time Hollywood pizzazz done up for women of today."

Kacey's head snapped up, her mouth open in surprise. "You hit the essence of my design concept right on the mark! Thanks for the compliment. You have a good eye for style," she told him. "I think I'm gonna like having you around."

Not as much as I'm gonna enjoy having you here, Leon thought, boldly raking Kacey with renewed appreciation. The afterbuzz of her remark fueled his sense that she was eager to explore whatever was developing between them. In her navy business attire, carefully coifed hair, shiny manicured nails and subtle, but stylish jewelry, she fit perfectly into the corporate image of a successful businesswoman. However, Leon could easily imagine what she would look like in the erotic red thong bikini that Truett was now dissecting on his computer-imaging machine. Even though she came off as the epitome of style, grace, good taste and high fashion, Leon suspected that underneath that crisp façade lurked a totally different woman, one who wore tight tank tops without a bra, stone-washed jeans without panties and was dying to break loose when she wasn't on the clock.

It sure would be fun to kick it with her while she's here, he mused as a rush of excitement swept through his body. The sudden surge of that heat settled low in his stomach, initiating the beginnings of an erection that took Leon by surprise. Quickly, he swiveled toward a desk and moved up close to shield himself from embarrassment.

What the hell was that about? He squared his shoulders, straightened his back and took a deep breath, knowing what was bothering him. His interest in Kacey Parker was quickly morphing into something more than professional, even though he knew better than to entertain such thoughts. He had to remember that she was still a city girl. Even her well-modulated voice screamed "East Coast Class," reminding Leon of how different they were. Though tempted, he worried about acting on the impulses that were hammering at his better judgment and creating a bulge in his pants. Getting personal with Kacey Parker might mess up his first big contract as the new owner of Archer Industries, disappointing his father—and himself.

Life in Rockport was slow, uncomplicated and casual, not at all like Kacey's, he imagined. But if she'd let him, he'd show her the upside of his hometown, as well as another side of himself—a side that he hadn't thought about sharing with anyone for a long, long time.

Chapter 7

The interior of the Seaside Suites was even drabber than Kacey had imagined it might be. A dark lobby filled with cheap furniture and a listless clerk who smelled of tobacco greeted her when she checked in.

After entering her room, Kacey tossed her suitcase onto the faded coverlet on the queen-size bed and then flopped into a pale green armchair by the window. She swept the room with a critical eye, appalled by the gaudy seashell motif that was plastered on every surface. Huge conch shells danced across blue wallpaper while flat white sand dollars dotted the deep red carpet. The clear glass bases of the bedside lamps were filled with a variety of tiny seashells, and the mirror over the dresser was framed with plastic replicas of various crustaceans, spray-painted bright golden yellow. Even the metal drawer pulls on the desk had been carved to resemble oyster husks.

Shaking her head in disbelief, Kacey turned her thoughts away from her dismal environment and back to the long, but rewarding day she'd had at Archer Industries. After working with Bob Truett to download all her patterns, she'd returned to her cubicle to make a few phone calls and finish some revisions. Leon had been very solicitous, almost too eager to make sure she was satisfied with the nips and tucks that Bob planned to make on the sample patterns. Before Leon left the building for a meeting in town he'd stopped by to give her his cell phone number in case she needed to talk to him.

Kacey had been both relieved and disappointed when Leon pulled out of the Archer parking lot with a squeal of tires and a flare of dust. She'd lingered at the window in her cubicle, watching the road long after his red Corvette had disappeared. The young Mr. Archer made her nervous as hell, but still, she liked the way he could put her at ease with only a smile. He made her heart race and her mouth go dry, yet she looked forward to being in the same room with him again tomorrow.

She had to admit it: Leon, the local playboy, had a lot going on. He drove a fiery red sports car, owned a house on the beach and clearly spared no expense to buy only the best of whatever he wanted. *Apparently, his family connections, good looks and magnetic personality must make him the most eligible bachelor in Rockport,* Kacey decided, imagining that Leon had probably romanced most of the available local women, and then some. Women who were only too happy to fawn over him, increasing his sense of self-importance. Women like Nona James.

The thought of Leon making love to Nona made Kacey flinch, though she knew she shouldn't give a hot damn about what he did or with whom. She had to settle her emotions, view Leon Archer Jr. as a professional colleague—nothing more. She had to concentrate on fabric choices and sample units, not the adorable way Leon tilted his head to the side when he looked at her or how seductively his torso tapered into his tight waist, creating perfect symmetry with his broad, muscular shoulders. Placing a hand to her stomach, Kacey sighed, trying to steady her nerves.

Tomorrow, the real work would begin as patterns hit the cutting boards and preparations for the first set of sample designs rolled forward. *That should keep my mind off Leon Archer's eyes, lips and his too fine butt.* At least for a while, she hoped, suddenly exhausted by the events of the day. All she wanted to do was take a hot shower, fall into bed and dream about ladies snatching her swimsuits off the racks inside Leeman's department stores.

When the thump-thump of a ball hitting the ground outside erupted, Kacey reached up, pulled the cord to open the mini blinds and peered into the courtyard of the apartment complex next door. She saw four young men racing around the well-worn asphalt lot, launching into a game of basketball. Their noisy play struck every nerve in Kacey's body, zapping her like jolts of electricity. The loud jeers and cheers as the boys called back and forth shattered the peace she had hoped to enjoy on her first night in Rockport.

"Oh, my God," Kacey groaned, quickly closing the

blinds. Was this a regular thing? Did the boys play there every evening? Annoyed, she grabbed the remote control off the desk and zapped the TV on, turning the volume up very loud in an attempt to drown out the ballplayers outside. However, her camouflage attempt prompted the person in the next room to pound on the wall and yell for her to turn the TV down. Clamping her teeth together, she bit back the urge to answer the knock with a pounding of her own, but lowered the volume, resigned to getting used to the noise coming from outside.

Why am I so edgy? she wondered. Living in the city, she was accustomed to the ever-present traffic noise and city sounds that rose up from the street and filtered into her third-floor apartment in Harlem. Why did it seem that, in Texas, everything was magnified and in her face—not as distant and impersonal as it was back home? Was it simply because she was in unfamiliar territory or because she was paying too much attention to her surroundings?

Either way, I don't think I'll ever get used to this place, she decided, reluctantly hanging her designer suits with matching blouses on wire hangers and placing her trendy pumps and sandals on the shabby carpet floor. Not knowing how long she'd be in Texas, she'd brought a good supply of clothing and shoes in order to be prepared for whatever might come up. She had several pairs of slacks and denim jeans. Capris matched with both dressy and casual tops. Sneakers. Her two favorite swimsuits and, of course, a generous supply of underwear and delicate lingerie.

As a teenager, Kacey had developed a passion for feminine, sexy underclothing and suspected that her love of these delicate items was what fostered her desire to create a swimwear line.

After arranging her toiletries and cosmetics on the ledge in the tiny bathroom, she stuck her empty suitcase on the top shelf of the closet and turned her thoughts to her next big decision: where to go for dinner.

She'd passed a pizza place and a cafeteria on her way to the motel, but neither choice struck her as particularly appealing, and she wasn't up for driving around hunting for a place to eat. In fact, she had no appetite at all.

Digging into her black patent Kate Spade tote, Kacey pulled out a plastic zipper bag containing tea bags, crackers, sweetener and packets of instant soup—the trusty emergency travel kit she never left home without. At least the Seaside Suites furnished a microwave oven and plastic cups. For tonight, that would have to do.

Leon parked his Corvette under the carport beside his house, turned off the engine and got out. As he walked along the sandy path leading to his back door, he admired the magnificent orange and gray sunset hovering just above the dark waters of the Gulf. The reflection of the sinking sun glimmering on the water turned the flat dusky expanse into a magical mirror weighted to the land. He climbed the steps leading up to his back deck and then paused, drinking in the sight that always greeted him. The only sounds that broke into his quiet cocoon were the gentle swish-swish of waves lapping at the shore and the occasional squawk of a seagull passing overhead.

Leon tossed his briefcase onto a canvas deck chair and leaned against the deck's polished wood rail, gazing out over the water. Though he'd grown up in his parents' huge traditional home and admired the old place with a passion, once he returned to Rockport after college and began to work for his father, he'd purchased and restored the dramatic one-story beach house that he now called home. It was the perfect place for him: he could be near the coastal waters that he loved so much, yet far enough away from the prying eyes of townsfolk and employees—who often took their familiarity with the Archer family too much to heart.

Born and raised in Rockport, Leon thought of himself as a country guy, content with small-town life—where everyone knew him and he fit right in. However, living in a place like Rockport, and being the only child of Mr. and Mrs. Archer, meant he belonged to the most influential and wealthy family in the city, a family that was respected and trusted by all.

The dramatic view from the wraparound deck that surrounded his house never failed to impress Leon, who had renovated the place with walls of glass on two sides, bringing the Gulf of Mexico right into his home. His nearest neighbor was one mile away and his location, far from the center of the city, was as close to perfect as could be appreciated. He could get to his mom and dad quickly in case of an emergency, yet he was far enough away to discourage impromptu visits.

After all, he *was* a bachelor, free to come and go as he pleased, and had no one to answer to but himself. Didn't he deserve to live in a luxurious seaside home that reflected his good taste and offered the privacy he craved? Leon took great pains to make his life as stress-free, and relationship-free, as possible, and at thirty-three he believed he had plenty of time before settling down to bring anyone else into his life. Until the urge to permanently bond with one particular woman hit him, he had no qualms about having as much fun as possible, while working as hard as he could.

The buzz of Leon's handheld interrupted his sunset watch. He checked the screen and grinned. It was Freddy, his longtime friend who lived in nearby Smithville, twenty miles inland from the coast.

"Hey, man. What's going on?" Leon answered, shoving his briefcase to the floor as he sat down in the deck chair.

"Everything," Freddy replied in his deeply melodious voice.

"Like?" Leon prompted, knowing Freddy well enough not to try to guess what he might be into at the moment. Freddy was a trust-fund baby with lots of cash, very little responsibility and a penchant for partying hard at the ranch he'd inherited from his parents.

"Got a call from Paul Grant…you remember him?" Freddy was saying.

"The rodeo dude who won all those medals—and cash—at the Houston Livestock show last year?"

"Yeah, that's the guy," Freddy confirmed.

"What about him?" Leon asked.

"He's bringing his crew and they're gonna put on a show here at the ranch weekend after next. Saturday *and* Sunday. It'll be the biggest roundup ever, man. Party time for real. I'm telling you, man. It's gonna be a blast. I've got folks coming in from as far away as Vegas to join in the fun. Booked a band. Top shelf liquor. Food for days. Girls galore. You've gotta come out for this one, bro. No kidding."

Leon hesitated, his mind spinning. When the close-knit atmosphere of life in Rockport became too claustrophobic and he needed to get away, Leon usually headed to Freddy's ranch, where he could drink beer, ride horses and hang out with his party buddies, who were ever-present at the ranch. At Freddy's ultramodern lodge in the semi-desert setting, the bar never closed, the stream of beautiful women never ended and the party never stopped. A weekend at Freddy's could chase away small-town blues and recharge Leon's batteries, increasing his appreciation of the quiet calm of Rockport when he returned.

"Sorry, wish I could, but I don't think I can make it," Leon told Freddy, adding the news that his father had just retired and turned the company over to him.

"All the more reason to celebrate, man. You don't wanna pass this one up."

The temptation to pack a bag and head to the ranch for a freewheeling good time challenged Leon's resistance. It would be a weekend trip. No need to worry about work. However, he knew he couldn't leave.

With a reluctant grimace, Leon told Freddy, "Sorry. Really. I'd better stick around here right now." Leon could sense his best friend's disappointment in the silence that hummed on the line. Rarely did Leon turn down one of Freddy's coveted invites, but this time it had to be done. "I've got a ton of work facing me, due to my dad's sudden retirement and all. Plus, I've got this designer in town…we have a contract to manufacture her swimsuit line. That's gonna take all my concentration."

"Can't Nona handle her?" Freddy quipped. "She knows as much about your dad's….uh, I mean, *your* company's operation as anybody."

"Naw, I promised Pop I'd handle this one personally,

and it's too important to leave with Nona, even though I know she could handle it."

"Okay, man. I hear you. Don't decide now. You've got time. Think about it."

"Okay," Leon agreed.

"Later," Freddy said, clicking off.

As the sunset gradually lost its luster, Leon remained on his deck, his thoughts centered on Kacey Parker. Suddenly, Freddy's invitation didn't strike him as very appealing. A wild rodeo weekend of drinking beer and partying wasn't what he wanted to do and he knew why. What he wanted to do was to stick around Rockport, get close enough to Kacey to see what made her tick. He had to find out if she was just a tease or if she was as stirred up as he was—if this crazy attraction he was feeling for her was on a two-way street.

Pushing up from his chair, Leon went inside and turned up the lights, illuminating the soft beige and gray décor of the interior of his house. The luster of chrome and glass contracted sharply with the warm tan walls and sectional that wrapped around a huge fireplace constructed of rough natural stone. Entering his golden granite kitchen, he went to the refrigerator and looked inside, suddenly very hungry. He grinned when he saw the large dish of lasagna, tossed salad and garlic bread that had been placed on the center shelf.

"Thank you, Mom," he murmured, knowing his mother, who loved to cook, must have dropped off the food while he was at work. Whenever she was about to leave town she always cooked up whatever was in her fridge and graciously donated her culinary creations to her son. *And it sure comes in on time tonight,* Leon thought, definitely too wired from his first day as owner of Archer Industries to begin to think about food.

Leon removed the casserole dish, set it on his kitchen counter and studied the oversized meal. *More than I can eat by myself,* he thought, as an idea began to form. Pulling out his cell phone he quickly dialed the number at the Seaside Suites Motel, his heart thumping crazily under his shirt.

Sitting with her back against the headboard of her too-soft bed, Kacey dunked a limp tea bag up and down in a cup of tepid water, and eyed the packet of crackers on her bedside table, resigned to eating her dreary meal alone. She settled in, took a sip from her cup and was just about to open the crackers when the room phone rang.

Startled, she nearly dropped the concoction that she was not looking forward to drinking. Reaching over, she picked up the receiver and answered, stunned, yet pleased to hear Leon's voice.

"Well, hello," she replied, determined to sound as if receiving a call from him was a perfectly natural thing.

"How's your room? Everything okay?" Leon asked.

"Oh, yes. It's fine," Kacey replied, thinking how nice it was of him to care about her comfort.

"Good. I was wondering if you'd had dinner," he asked right off.

Kacey laughed aloud, giving up a soft giggle that let him know he'd struck a chord. "Uh…if you can call a cup of lukewarm herbal tea and slightly stale crackers dinner, then yes."

Leon groaned in disgust. "How does homemade lasagna with hot garlic bread sound?"

"Heavenly." A beat. "So you cook, too, huh?"

"Naw. Compliments of my mom. She loves to feed me."

"All right. Sooo…are you inviting me to dinner?"

"Absolutely."

"I accept."

"I'll pick you up in fifteen minutes."

Chapter 8

From the road, Leon's home resembled an ordinary ranch house, with a low-slung profile, sleek horizontal windows and a tall brick chimney rising high above the roofline in the middle of the structure. However, as Kacey soon discovered, behind the building's rather nondescript façade was a fabulous home with a beach view that blew her mind.

After parking his Corvette under the carport, Leon walked with Kacey along the sandy path that led to the back entrance of the house. Her mouth dropped open in shock at the sight that greeted her. The entire rear of Leon's home was wrapped with a true mahogany deck that offered a spectacular view of the Gulf of Mexico. The tropical landscape leading down to the water resembled a cushy mat of lush green foliage punctuated by succulent blooming cacti and prickly heat-hardy plants. Nestled within the unusual, and intriguing, garden were bubbling fountains with cascades of silvery water where solar lights twinkled among the exotic flowering shrubs. The scent of salt water, mingled with jasmine, perfumed the air and pulled Kacey deeper into her fascination with Leon, as well as his private escape.

"What a fantastic place," she commented, mounting the steps to the deck, where a patio table had been draped with a white cloth and set with plates for dinner for two.

"Thanks. I like it, too," Leon replied as he lifted the glass hurricane shade in the center of the table and lit the thick white candle beneath it, shielding the flame from the brisk coastal winds with a cup of his hand. The light quickly shed a shimmer of gold over the gilt-rimmed wineglasses waiting to be filled and created a twinkle of amber light on plates that reflected the starry sky overhead.

"It's not too cool for you out here, is it?" he asked.

"Not at all. This is heaven, after all the cold rain in New York." Moving to stand at the deck's rail, Kacey stared out over the dark, wave-crested water, taking in the surreal scene. In the distance, a slow-moving private yacht drifted past, looking like a holiday sparkler with its tiny windows all ablaze. Beyond the pleasure boat, she spied a much larger vessel that broke the line of the horizon in a hulking oblong shadow.

"That's a cruise ship bound for Mexico," Leon told her before she had a chance to ask. "They pass by on a regular schedule. I could set my watch by the Kings Cruise ships. Very punctual line."

"How serene," Kacey remarked, parting her lips to

suck in a breath of sea air, loving the feel of the gentle breeze that caressed her face and ruffled the white linen tablecloth.

"Yes, it is peaceful," Leon agreed, reaching for the bottle of wine on the table. "Is red okay?" he asked, lifting up the bottle. "Produced in a local winery."

Kacey turned to face Leon, struck silent by a catch in her throat that held her words in check. Was it only this morning that she'd been grumbling about going to Rockport, feeling resentful about being stuck in Texas? Now, all she wanted to do was linger on this fantastic deck and drink wine with this handsome man until the sun came up. Why was her mind stuck on how damn handsome Leon Archer was and how quickly he was moving into her heart? It all seemed so fast...so surreal, yet so right. Was she complaining? Not at all. In fact, Kacey knew she wanted nothing more than for Leon Archer to make the first move. And after that, well, she wasn't sure *what* might happen, but she damn sure wanted to find out.

Kacey gave Leon a quick nod and smiled as he removed the cork from the wine bottle, poured two glasses and then moved next to her. She accepted the drink, cupping her fingers around the bowl of the glass as she tasted the wine. "Very nice."

"Good. I think so, too."

"And you said this is local?" she asked, impressed by the smooth, silky taste of the wine.

"Yep. The winery is not far from here." He placed a hand on her shoulder and pointed toward the east. "Just over that ridge. Where the land rises up at that jagged tree line. That's the vineyard. A beautiful piece of land."

"I've never drunk Texas wine," she admitted. Then she added, "In fact, I'd never thought about Texas as a place where wine was produced."

Leon chuckled. "You're not alone. But the word is getting out. More local growers are planting grapes instead of cotton. Something to tell your city friends about when you return home," Leon stated.

"For sure. I'm impressed with your hometown. What else should I know?"

"That we have real rodeo competitions around here."

"Rodeo? You mean roping steers and riding cows?" Kacey asked.

Leon sputtered in laughter. "Steers, horses and bulls get ridden, but not cows," he clarified. "Yes. It's true. There's a very active rodeo circuit in these parts," he told Kacey. "A friend of mine owns a ranch in Smithville— about twenty miles from here. His grandparents founded the oldest black rodeo in the state. In fact, he's hosting a pretty well-known rodeo crew weekend after next."

"Hmm…fascinating. I've never seen a rodeo," Kacey admitted.

"Really? I think you'd like it. I could take you if…"

"If I'm still here," Kacey finished with a lift of an eyebrow. "We might be finished with my line by then."

"You'll be here," Leon stated with such assurance that it sent a shiver of anticipation curling tightly around Kacey's heart.

"You love this part of the country, don't you?" Kacey said, her voice soft and sincere.

"Yeah, I do. I know this is not a very lively town, but Rockport's not bad at all. It's small, but a good place to live. Don't think I'd want to live anywhere else," Leon added.

After a short pause and another sip of wine, Kacey set her glass on the deck rail and leaned into the fragrant breeze. "I see why. You're a very lucky man."

"Lucky?" he repeated, questioning her remark. "I don't know if I'd use that word to describe me."

"Really, it's true," Kacey insisted. "Sounds like you have a very solid life here. You have a secure family business, you have a wonderful home and your parents are close by, too."

"Are yours?" he asked, voice low.

Kacey grew quiet, swallowed and then told Leon, "No. I'm an only child, like you, but my mom and dad divorced when I was ten. Now, she lives in Florida and my dad is in Seattle. I talk to them on holidays and birthdays, but we're not all that close."

"Sorry," Leon said. "I guess that's tough."

Kacey shrugged. "It's just the way things are. You have your own slice of paradise right here, and I have a tiny apartment in Harlem," she stated, tracing the angles of Leon's face, which glowed like hammered bronze in the candlelight. "This place is so beautiful and different from the rest of Rockport, especially the motel, which leaves a lot to be desired," she remarked, slowly twirling her wineglass, her attention on the water.

"Yeah, I guess the Seaside Suites is definitely not the best representative of Rockport."

"Amen to that," Kacey concurred. "After I checked into my room, I have to admit that I was beginning to regret coming here. It is so drab and depressing. And a bunch of rowdy boys use the parking lot next door to play basketball. The people in the room next to mine pound on the walls if I turn up the volume on my TV." She chuckled, and then added, "I wasn't feeling very impressed with your city earlier tonight."

Leon grimaced. "I hate to think of you being unhappy or depressed."

"Don't worry about me. I came here to work. I'll manage just fine."

"I'm sure you will," Leon countered. "But I hope you'll let me help make things a bit more comfortable for you."

"You already have," Kacey admitted, as casually as she could, tensing her fingers around the stem of her glass and silently counting to ten. "Your invitation to dinner came right on time. Got me out of the motel so I could enjoy this wonderful view of the Gulf, and I'm especially looking forward to the fabulous dinner you promised."

Leon's eyes widened. "Yes, dinner! It's in the oven heating up. Won't be long, I promise. In the meantime, tell me more about yourself and your work. You strike me as someone who has big plans and does not give up very easily."

"Really? What do you base that on?" Kacey pressed, surprised by Leon's comment and wanting to hear why he'd said that.

"Oh, just the fact that you're launching your own line of swimsuits is impressive enough. Not everyone can do that."

"Well, it's something I've wanted to do for a long time, and it feels great to finally be on the verge of pulling it off."

Leon lifted his wineglass. "How about a toast to SunKissed by Kacey?" he offered.

Kacey beamed her appreciation at Leon, grateful for his obvious desire to make sure her dream came off without a hitch. "I'll drink to that…and to a successful stay in Rockport," she added, finding the idea of working with Leon, and spending more personal time with him, very appealing.

"Definitely," Leon remarked as they clinked glasses, sipped and then locked eyes. "Kacey, I want you to know that I plan to do all I can to make sure your time here is well worth it. I know leaving New York to oversee the production of your swimsuit line was probably not something you wanted to do. But it will pay off, I promise. My first responsibility to you, and Leeman's, is to manufacture a product that meets your expectations, and I take that very seriously. However, I also feel responsible for your experience while you're in Rockport."

Kacey watched Leon closely, keenly aware of the double meaning in his words, feeling challenged by his admission that he planned to commit personal time to her outside of their working relationship.

"I want to make sure you leave my hometown with good memories," he added.

"Starting with tonight, I assume?" Kacey murmured, her voice drifting off into the wind.

"Absolutely," he replied, moving a step closer. "It started as soon as you accepted my invitation."

"Because I was desperate to be rescued from a pitiful excuse of a meal alone in my room."

"Exactly! I came to your rescue, so…I guess you have to call me your hero?" he taunted with a grin.

"My hero?" she quipped, letting Leon know that she

was happy to banter with him as they got to know each other.

"Absolutely," Leon countered. "As long as you're in Rockport, I plan to make sure you're never bored…or lonely again. That is, if you'll let me," he finished, his words thick with hope.

Kacey tensed to hear the tenderness in his promise, and knew he was tempting her to make a decision. Should she allow this personal connection to deepen? Had she already gone too far by coming to his home? Should she step back, clear her head and resolve to keep everything between them strictly business? Knowing that the prospect of having a romantic relationship with Leon was actually not that far-fetched, Kacey hesitated to speak. The guy was handsome. Smart. Obviously attracted to her. And she was definitely melting under his intense steel-gray gaze.

Why not go for it? she thought, her eyes tracing over his features as he waited for her to say something. So far, he had not offered to take her inside his house—which was fine with her. A friendly dinner outside on his patio and a quick ride back to the motel was the best way to handle their first encounter away from the office. Wasn't it?

However…I'll only be in town a short time. I might as well have an experience worth sharing with Linette, who always has exciting, outrageous things happen to her when she's working a photo shoot. This time, Kacey would have a juicy story of her own to dish when they went for drinks on a Friday happy hour.

"I just might take you up on that. I'd be happy to call you my hero," she jokingly confessed, looking forward to finding out what Leon had in mind. However, the pensive glimmer in his eyes told Kacey that he was dead serious about lavishing his hospitality on her and extending their relationship beyond its business borders. Fine, because she was more than ready for the grand Texas adventure he was offering.

And it's already started, she recognized, deciding that jumping all the way in was the best way to find out just how strong her attraction to Leon Archer was, and how dangerously close he'd come to capturing her heart.

When Leon leaned over and brushed his lips over Kacey's, the gesture did not surprise her, offend her or make her want to run away. When her tongue sprang to life and twined lazily with his, he opened his mouth wider to intensify the connection. Kacey felt her limbs go weak when his arms came up and encircled her. She sank against him, relaxing as if she'd been in his embrace many times before. When he snaked his hands down and clasped them together in the hollow of her back, she let him guide her to a deck post and brace her back against it. Sealed together, their lips and arms were so tightly locked that Kacey could hardly breathe. However, letting Leon go did not cross her mind as she held him in place and accepted the flurry of kisses that he placed on her cheeks, her neck, the hollow of her throat.

When they finally came up for air, Leon groaned, shifted to place his hip against the deck rail and sat sideways as he gazed at Kacey. "You're so beautiful, standing here with the candlelight behind you. I couldn't resist."

Kacey gave him a languid blink, recovering from their kiss, feeling buoyant, yet grounded in her decision to explore the explosive chemistry that was rapidly building between them.

"I could hold you, kiss you, forever," he murmured, reaching up to touch her chin with a finger.

"Not forever, I hope. And let me starve to death?" Kacey joked, desperate to defuse the awkward aftermath of that too serious, too soon, too damn delicious kiss!

With a jolt, Leon stood and gaped at the house. "Damn! The food! It's on its way. Wait. You sit down. I'll be right back." He dashed into the kitchen, which Kacey could see was right off the deck, leaving her laughing as he fled to the oven.

Within moments, Leon returned carrying a steaming casserole dish, the smell of pungent lasagna drifting out before him.

Seated at the table on the deck, they chatted easily over a dinner of the best lasagna Kacey had ever eaten, paired with a tangy Italian salad, cheesy garlic bread and the local red wine that rivaled any produced in California.

After the meal, Leon stood up and picked up his plate. Kacey quickly assisted in clearing the table.

"Come on inside," he invited, starting toward the house. "I can use your help cleaning up."

"Oh, yeah?" Kacey quipped. "So that's the only reason you're inviting me inside?"

Turning to face her, he grinned. "No, of course not. I'd love to show you the rest of the house. You don't have to leave right away, do you?"

As Kacey stared at Leon, her mind was flooded with all the reasons she should tell him, *I really can't stay long. I need to get back to the motel and far away from temptation.* However, her legs paid no attention to such rational thinking as she followed him inside.

Leon's once-modest ranch house had been renovated into a surprisingly open floor plan with few walls to obscure its dramatic views of the Gulf. Sleek modern furnishings, contemporary art and walls painted in subdued shades of tan and gray welcomed Kacey, who saw that Leon's sophisticated décor compared favorably with any cushy Manhattan penthouse. Brushed nickel and glass tables, sleek black and white marble statues on mirrored pedestals and oversized rugs in geometric patterns completed the updated interior that felt open and airy, yet comfortably intimate. His spacious bedroom was done in an African safari theme, with gorgeous prints of exotic animals on the walls and luxurious bedding that added to the wildly exotic theme.

After the tour of the house, they did the dishes and then settled at the kitchen bar, more glasses of wine in hand. At Leon's urging, Kacey gave him a quick overview of what growing up in the bustling community of Harlem had been like, and then he described his small town upbringing in Rockport, where his family's roots went back four generations.

They communicated in an easy, friendly way that made all of Kacey's earlier apprehension vanish. All she wanted at that moment was to stay there with Leon and delve deeper into the life of this man who was pushing all her buttons with such grace and ease.

Chapter 9

For five minutes straight, Nona focused on the clock above her kitchen sink, wondering what Leon was doing. Certainly, he was at home by now, alone, and hopefully enjoying the lasagna she'd baked and delivered to his house—just as his mother would have done.

After rinsing the single plate, glass and fork Nona had used for her own dinner of spaghetti and meatballs, she placed the dishes in the drying rack and hung her towel on its bar, her thoughts locked on Leon in a particularly insistent way.

She was proud of herself for accepting his mother's request to look after the plants and her fish—things Mrs. Archer cared deeply about. And that certainly included her son, didn't it? The trust Mrs. Archer placed in Nona made her heart swell with satisfaction.

Knowing that Leon loved his mom's lasagna, Nona

had taken great pains to hone the family recipe, just as she worked on honing her relationship with Mrs. Archer, who treated Nona like a daughter.

"And one day, *daughter-in-law,*" she murmured, a wave of desire sweeping through her body. She had known Leon almost all her life. She'd lost her virginity to him at Barker's Bend when she was sixteen years old, and was convinced that she and Leon were destined to be together. However, their ultimate union was taking longer than Nona had ever expected it would and she was growing impatient. For so many years she had stood on the sidelines, watching while Leon raced from one disastrous romantic relationship to another. His frantic desire to play the local playboy was starting to wear on her nerves. How much longer could she remain in the shadows, steadfastly supportive of him, offering an ear primed to listen to his troubles as each of his misguided relationships fell by the wayside?

Leon's getting older every day. I am, too. He needs to get his act together and stop playing the field. Those days are about to be over for him. It's time he settled down, got married and started his family, she reassured herself. And since he was at that point in his life, wasn't she the woman he ought to turn to? Didn't she understand him better than anyone? Didn't she have his parents' blessing as the hometown girl who'd grown up with him and knew what made him tick? Though they hadn't had sex since they were in high school, she knew what pleased Leon sexually, and was more than ready to prove it.

It's just a matter of time, Nona told herself, her ever-recurring fantasy of living with Leon in his fantastic house on the beach rising up to swamp her mind. Her favorite part of the fantasy was imagining how beautiful their children would be, with her smooth, light brown skin and his startling gray eyes. The image made her shiver with anticipation and delight.

Overwhelmed by a need to hear his voice, Nona dried her hands on a towel and reached for the green plastic phone on her wall. Feeling smugly possessive, she punched in Leon's number, roused by the delicious quiver of longing that contracted the walls of her dormant womanhood.

"Hello?" Leon answered, irritated to be interrupted just when things between Kacey and him were beginning to warm up. He'd made the right move, inviting her to dinner, and he'd been on target about her interest in getting together with him outside the office, too.

I damn sure know how to read a woman, he thought smugly, smothering a smile and looking forward to spending as much time as he could with Kacey. However, the prospect of her leaving Rockport hung like a dark shadow in the back of Leon's mind. He'd have to deal with that eventually, but for now, he planned to show her a good time and enjoy her company, proving to her that his hometown could be as good a place, or better, than New York City. Oh, yes, and he planned to produce a swimsuit line that would bring her rave reviews.

"How was it?" Nona asked Leon, pressing her voice through the line and forcing his attention back to the phone call.

"What are you calling about?" Leon asked, adopting a cool, businesslike tone to let Nona know that he was not up for one of her rambling treks back into ancient history. When she was lonely, depressed or had drunk too much brandy, she called—mumbling on and on about their high school days until she ran out of steam. Though he had been involved with her when he was a teenager, he now thought of her more like a sister, one on whom he could never turn his back. But all that stuff she liked to talk about was just a bunch of dusty memories, better off forgotten. They'd both moved on since then. At least he had. He wasn't so sure about Nona. However, one thing was clear: he had to stop accommodating her pity parties, even though he hated to cut her off. She always made him feel obligated to listen, and was quick to remind him that his mom and hers had been best friends forever.

"Duh! How was the lasagna that I made for you?" Nona shot back. "Was it as good as your mom's?"

Leon stilled, his mind processing what Nona was telling him, and not liking what he'd heard. "Could you clarify that?" he asked, shrugging at Kacey while mouthing the words, *Nona—something about an order,* wanting to keep her out of this mess. As much as he genuinely liked and trusted his longtime friend, at times Nona could be a pain in the ass. The last thing he needed was a dose of her overprotective mothering to spoil the romantic mood he was attempting to create with Kacey.

"Oh, it was your mom's suggestion," Nona was saying. "She gave me her keys and asked me to kinda keep an eye on her plants and feed her fish while she and Mr. Archer were away."

"Oh, now I understand," Leon stated, forcing a calm vibe into his carefully chosen words. *And you thought that included feeding me?* he silently fumed, irritated as hell that Nona would assume she had the right to use the key he had given to his mother to do what she did.

"There's no need for that," he said, desperate to sound as if he and Nona were talking about work.

"Oh, I know. But it would make your mom happy to know that I'm making sure you eat well. So I made the lasagna and brought it over this afternoon while you were at your meeting."

"I wish you had said something to me about this at the office," Leon quipped. Damn! He loved his mother but he didn't like the way she doted on Nona. His mom might want Nona James for a daughter-in-law, but Leon sure as hell had no intention of ever making good on that far-fetched wish.

"No need. I just hope it was good," Nona replied in a whispery voice.

"It was," he said, his mind fishing for the perfect way to end Nona's interruption. A long pause, and then Leon tossed out the zinger that he knew would bring silence to the other end of the line. "You know, I'm sitting here talking to *Kacey* about that right now," he launched, eager to send Nona the message that he was not alone and he did not have time to talk.

"Oh? Kacey Parker is there?" Nona snapped, sounding disappointed.

"Right," Leon answered.

"Uh, then I guess you can't talk, huh?"

"Right again."

"Okay, then. I'll see you at the office tomorrow," Nona finished in a dispirited murmur.

"Yes. We'll finish discussing this at the office," Leon said, quickly ending the call.

"Is everything okay?" Kacey asked, once Leon had clicked off.

Composing his expression, he erased the frown

creasing his brow and took a deep breath, giving Kacey a look that let her know nothing urgent was going on. He certainly didn't want Kacey to know that Nona was calling about some stupid prank she'd pulled. A prank that did not please him at all.

"Oh, nothing important. Nona had a question about a work order." He hated to lie about something as inconsequential as a dish of lasagna, but Nona's call left him worried. She was treading too close to his personal life, and it had to stop. But how could he push back without offending her? How could he convince Nona that she'd overstepped her boundaries, when his parents were always treating her as if she were a permanent fixture in the family? He'd told his mom and dad time and time again that he had no intention of ever marrying Nona, but they paid no attention, stuck on the fact that Nona James was the hometown girl he was destined to settle down with—the woman who would stand by him and help him run the family business, just as his mother had done with his father.

They just don't understand, Leon silently complained, wondering what they would think and how they would react if he brought a sophisticated woman like Kacey Parker home to meet them.

Nona slung herself into the frayed red recliner that faced her ash-filled fireplace, stretched out her legs and squeezed back tears. *Why is Leon wasting his time with that citified designer?* she silently asked herself, her teeth clamped together tightly in despair. *She might be pretty, but she's an outsider who will never fit in here. Leon needs me. I need him. We understand each other.*

Chapter 10

Kacey's second day in Rockport started with an early morning phone call. The ringing sound brought a smile to her lips as she reached across her bed to answer. *Leon,* was her first thought, prompting vivid images of their evening together. Their romantic dinner on the deck. The quiet way they had talked about their careers and their lives over wine in his kitchen. The ride back to the motel with the convertible top down and soft jazz playing in the car. And then, the good-night kiss that had created a connection that left her sizzling with desire and her nipples as hard as tiny pebbles on the beach.

Grabbing the phone, Kacey whispered a sexy hello, only to have her fantasy shattered when she heard Ariana Mendio's voice barking a too-loud greeting over the line.

"Oh, hi, Ariana," Kacey said, sitting up to brace her

back against the headboard and push visions of Leon's lean hard body tangled among animal print sheets on his king-size bed from her mind. Hoping to sound alert and very much on top of things, she strengthened her voice when she commented, "You're on the job early, huh?"

"Early?" Ariana threw out. "It's seven-thirty in New York."

Kacey looked at the clock. "And six-thirty here."

"Ah, so it is," Arian admitted, as if it really didn't matter. "I need an update on everything. Hadley wants daily reports. I'll be calling every day…early. Before you get into your day."

"Well, you've certainly done that," Kacey commented, a tad irritated to learn how closely Hadley planned to track her activity. He'd never done that before. But she shouldn't be surprised. He was taking a great risk in green-lighting her line and she knew he expected nothing less than perfect results.

"What do you want to know first?" Kacey inquired, deciding it would be best to let Ariana ask for what she wanted rather than try to relate every detail of her time at Archer Industries so far.

"Well, how did your first encounter with Archer go? You and the old man getting along?"

A wry chuckle flew from Kacey's lips, erasing her annoyance with Ariana's early-morning phone call. "I haven't even met Mr. Archer," Kacey informed her coworker.

"What? Why not?" Ariana's voice rose one octave below a screech.

"Because he's in Africa," Kacey coolly teased.

"Africa? What's going on?"

"Calm down," Kacey advised, proceeding to tell Ariana about the sudden change in ownership at Archer and that Leon Archer Jr. was now in charge.

"Really? I'm surprised that Leon Sr. stepped down. He didn't seem like the type who would ever let go."

"Well, there comes a time for change in every situation," Kacey commented, thinking about how quickly her feelings for Leon had morphed into something she was still trying to figure out. "Guess it was my lucky day to arrive when change came to this place."

"So, what's young Mr. Archer like?" Ariana asked.

Sexy. Magnetic. Intriguing, Kacey wanted to say, still basking in the afterglow of their evening together. *A tall, brown tower of a man who is creeping under my skin and into my heart.*

However, instead of confessing her fast-growing attraction to Leon, she hastily composed a more acceptable response. "He's very helpful. Dedicated to making our line a smashing success, and completely confident that we'll bring SunKissed in on time and on budget."

"That's all we care about," Ariana blithely agreed. "Hadley gave me your revised projections. Everything looks good. However, there's not a second to waste. I'm starting the promotional campaign today. I have to line up models for the test photo shoot and book the photographer. When will the samples arrive?"

"Oh, about that," Kacey stammered, biting her bottom lip as she studied the seashells in the base of her bedside lamp, concerned. She had not informed Hadley about her decision to make the samples in her size, and it was too late to revise her plan. Truett had already adjusted the patterns and they planned to start cutting today.

"I decided to change things a bit," Kacey began. "I'm

going to shoot the samples here in Rockport. I called Linette…she can fly in from LA to do it."

"Kacey," Ariana responded in a throaty growl that conveyed her obvious displeasure. "That's not going to work. No, no, no. Hadley will never agree to fly all the models to Texas just for the test-shoot. What are you thinking? You know how closely he's monitoring the money. We can't blow a bundle on airfare and all the expense to do that, please. Just FedEx the samples to me when they're ready."

"Don't worry, Ariana. I don't want the models to come to Texas. My plan won't increase the budget. In fact, it'll reduce it."

"How? Explain, please."

"I'm having the samples made to fit *me*…and I'll be the model that Linette can shoot. Okay?" The silence that stretched between Texas and New York let Kacey know she'd dropped a bombshell that was about to explode.

"Crazy!"

"No, it's not. I can save the company time and money," she defended, eager to defuse the situation and keep Ariana on her side. "This would only be for the manufacturer's samples, just to see how the colors and styles photograph. When we get to the final takes for the website and the brochures, we'll use the models, and we can shoot the catalog pics in the studio in New York. Just as we always do, okay?"

"Well, maybe," Ariana hedged, not sounding fully convinced. "You know, I really don't care if you want to model your swimsuits. What I want is for you to stay on target as far as final delivery is concerned."

Mentally clicking through her tightly arranged

schedule, Kacey reviewed her time frame with Ariana. "The patterns have been adjusted. All the fabric is in, even the Naughty Net should arrive tomorrow."

"I hope so, since the see-through-when-wet piece is a featured style."

"If all goes well, I think we can have everything finalized and start full production sooner than I'd hoped."

"All right," Ariana agreed. "I'll be checking in every day. I'm counting on you to deliver, Kacey. Don't let me down."

"I won't," Kacey promised, sensing the weight of her responsibilities more than ever.

Flinging back the bed sheet, she went into the bathroom to take a shower and get ready for the day. Standing under the stream of warm water, she rotated her head from side to side, loosening the tension that had gathered in her neck during her exchange with Ariana, whose phone call had put Kacey on notice: there was a lot to accomplish in a very short time frame, and she didn't dare stray off course. Kacey had come to Rockport with only one desire—to see her swimsuit line to completion. But could she deny that Leon Archer was quickly rearranging her list of priorities and it didn't bother Kacey in the least?

Dressed in black raw linen slacks, a deep-cuffed white silk shirt and gladiator sandals with just enough heel to increase her height without making her look overdressed for the office, Kacey sat down at her desk. However, immediately after settling into her cubicle at Archer Industries, everything went dark, plunging the factory into silence. The chatter of employees immediately dropped off. The buzz of ringing telephones died and the hum of machinery ground to a halt. Though startled by the blackout, Kacey didn't panic. She'd experienced blackouts, brownouts and unexpected electrical blips many times in the city, and knew that, usually, the problem was resolved very quickly. However, the prospect of any delay in the work she planned to accomplish today made her nervously tap her fingers on the arm of her chair as she waited for the lights to come back on. The last thing she needed was a power failure to throw her off schedule, searing her pledge to Ariana more deeply into her mind.

From out in the corridor, Kacey heard Leon reassuring his staff that everything was under control. "The power company is here," he was saying. "They'll get everything up and running as soon as possible. No need to panic. Just stay where you are."

Kacey smiled to herself. He sounded very calm, in control and steady, creating a sense of safety that was comforting. No wonder his employees were so loyal to him.

Leon stuck his head into Kacey's workspace and handed her a flashlight. Looking up at him she felt her heart lurch when his seductive gray eyes locked on hers, sending her whirling back in time—to the night before as they stood together on the candlelit deck, testing each other's will to deny the attraction that was clearly binding them together.

The ring of Leon's cell phone shattered her reminiscence, but she kept her eyes trained on him as he answered.

"Any idea how long we'll be down?" he asked his caller.

Kacey raised a brow and waited until he'd finished before asking him the same thing.

"Longer than I'd hoped," Leon told her, scowling with regret. He squinted into the light that Kacey leveled on his face. "That was the power company. The transmitter behind the plant exploded. Has to be replaced."

"How long will that take?"

"Most of the day," Leon replied, clearly unhappy about the situation. "Which means I have to shut down the plant and send everybody home."

"What about backup generators?" Lacey inquired, searching for a way to keep going. In New York, many private residences and companies maintained a second source of power for situations like this.

"We do have several I could fire up, however, they'd only keep the ceiling lights and air conditioners going. Not strong enough to run industrial machinery for very long."

Kacey glumly nodded her understanding, swallowing the unease that swept through her at this unexpected delay.

"Don't look so anxious," Leon reassured her, stepping deeper into her cubicle. "I know you're worried about the schedule, but we can make up for today and still meet your deadline—I promise."

Within the circle of light coming from her flashlight, Kacey watched as Leon extended his hand toward her, as if trying to touch her arm in reassurance. She surprised herself by stepping closer, eager for his overture of comfort, yet feeling somewhat ashamed of herself for allowing him to see how much she wanted to feel his hands on her once again.

In the dim room, their bodies swayed together, as if

drawn like magnets toward wills of steel. Leon touched Kacey on the shoulder, and then moved his hand up to her cheek, where he slid his thumb along her chin. "If we were anyplace other than here at the plant, I'd switch off this flashlight and kiss the hell out of you."

His remark sent a flare of arousal straight into Kacey's core, heating her up and making her want to feel more than his hands on her body. Surrounded by darkness, his sensuous remark slid into her heart and created a quirky mix of danger and desire that she had never felt before. Knowing his bold declaration required a bold comeback, she jumped right in to deliver.

"If we were anyplace other than here at the plant, I just might let you," she stated, fully aware of what might happen and totally at ease with the hardness of his manhood when it suddenly pressed against her leg.

Leon slowly eased his hand down the side of her neck and onto her shoulder, which he squeezed in reassurance before inching closer. "Then maybe we need to go someplace else?" he huskily suggested.

"Like where?" she teased, excited by the idea of tumbling totally into this blinding flash of desire that threatened to consume her.

"Several places come to mind, but let me think this over."

"Go on…. I'm game."

"Okay, since we can't work today, how does a tour of my hometown sound?"

"Might be nice," she confessed, truly interested in seeing more of the area.

"Okay. Stay put. I'll be right back," he said, beaming his flashlight out into the hallway. "I have to release everyone for the rest of the day and secure the plant. Is your cell phone on?" he inquired, breaking the tension that wired the room like an unseen electrical grid.

Shining her flashlight onto her purse, Kacey located her cell phone and pressed it on. "It is now," she said.

"Good, what's your number?" he asked, punching it into his phone as she rattled it off. "All set. I'll call you from outside as soon as I get everything under control. Keep your phone handy." Then he disappeared into the dark corridor, his footsteps echoing through the building, leaving Kacey staring after him.

"I am crazy as hell," she admonished herself, swallowing the spurt of longing that had risen in her throat and engulfed her during their brief encounter. *I'll be right here when you come back, and hopefully, after my hometown tour, we can pick up where we left off, and in a more private location, too.*

Standing alone in the dark, Kacey prayed she was not making a huge mistake by allowing Leon to get so personal with her. But she couldn't help herself. She was mesmerized by his sensual personality, entranced by his gentleness, already addicted to his kisses and far too eager to explore the sexual tension that jumped to life the moment their eyes met.

However, as much as she wanted Leon Archer as a man, she still had business to take care of. With the production of her line at stake, any delay was unacceptable. But all she really *could* do was trust Leon and work with him to make up for lost time.

Placing the flashlight on her desk, Kacey sank into her chair, her heart thudding in question. As irritated as she was about the blackout, she had to admit that she wanted to be alone with Leon, to let him touch her in places that yearned to feel his fingertips, his lips, his hands. What she longed for was a chance to relive the shivers of delight that had swept through her when he'd held her close last night.

"What's wrong with me?" she fretted, unnerved by the conflicting emotions assaulting her in the dark. Desperate for a reality check, she impulsively pressed Linette's phone number into her cell, eager to spill all to her girlfriend and get her take on what had transpired since her arrival in Rockport. However, after punching in the number, Kacey disconnected the call after the first ring. It was early morning on the West Coast. Linette, who was always groggy in the morning, would be furious with her for calling at the crack of dawn.

Setting her phone aside, Kacey tried to relax, though she felt as if she were about to explode. What she needed was a way to release all this pent-up energy and unfulfilled desire. What she needed was for Leon Archer to come back and finish what he'd started.

Chapter 11

Nona moved quietly down the corridor toward Kacey's cubicle, shining her flashlight along the carpeted floor. Having decided that sticking close to the woman whom Leon had obviously targeted as his next romantic conquest would be the best way to stay on top of whatever was going on, Nona was on a mission. She'd play the cooperative coworker, gain the designer's trust and, hopefully, get Kacey to open up about whatever was going on between her and Leon. Having been through too many of Leon's casual flirtations to count, Nona had no doubt that this lopsided romance would be short-lived because those two had absolutely nothing in common.

"You okay in there?" Nona asked, stepping into Kacey's cubicle and shining her light all around.

"Oh! Yes. Hello, Nona," Kacey replied, blinking into the sudden beam that illuminated the room.

"Just thought I'd check," Nona offered, settling against the doorframe, her eyes focused on Kacey. "I was worried about you, being unfamiliar with the plant and all."

"Thanks for your concern. It is kinda creepy sitting here in the dark," Kacey replied in a voice that let Nona know she was glad to have some company.

"I just spoke to Leon. He told me to tell you it'll be empty around here real soon. Want me to walk out with you?"

"No, but thanks. Leon asked me to wait here for him," Kacey replied. "But I appreciate your offer. I just hope this power outage will be resolved by tomorrow."

"Oh, probably so," Nona replied casually. Not about to be dismissed so easily, Nona sat down across from Kacey, ready for business. She was still seething over the fact that this woman had shared the meal she'd prepared especially for Leon. No need to play hide-and-seek with her. "How'd things go last night?" Nona inquired, tilting her head to one side and allowing an explosion of natural curls to cover one eye.

"Last night? Uh…okay, I guess. The motel was kind of noisy and that apartment complex next door is…"

"I wasn't referring to the Seaside Suites," Nona interrupted coolly. "I mean with you and Leon…at his house." Nona bit back the smile that threatened to erupt at the stunned expression that claimed Kacey's features. Clearly, she was rattling the designer, and that was exactly what she'd hoped to do.

"Oh, right. Leon and I had a very nice time," Kacey replied. "I was glad that he rescued me from a meal of weak tea and crackers at the motel. We were outside on the deck and enjoyed the night breeze off the water. I loved his house. He has a very beautiful home."

"I know," Nona deadpanned. "I've been there hundreds of times." A short pause before she said, "And how was the lasagna?" Nona let the slightest wrinkle of a self-satisfied grin tug her upper lip when Kacey's jaw went slack in surprise. *You might be a fancy designer, and think you know so much but you don't know anything at all,* she mused, crossing her arms as she took in Kacey's reaction.

"He told you what we had to eat, too?" Kacey remarked, shifting to one side, clearly uneasy over Nona's knowledge of such details. "The lasagna was delicious. The best I've ever had, I think."

"Thanks. I appreciate that. Guess I've finally perfected Mrs. Archer's recipe. Been working at it for a while."

"What? You mean, *you* made the lasagna?" Kacey snapped forward, squinting at Nona in the beam of light trained on her face.

"I sure did. Didn't Leon tell you I made dinner for him?"

"No, he didn't." Kacey's words were tinged with ice.

"Must have slipped his mind," Nona commented coolly. Slumping back in her chair, she focused on a far wall, allowing memories to surge forward and fill her mind. "When Leon and I were younger, his mother used to invite me over to his house on Friday nights to give me cooking lessons. You see, my mom died when I was twelve years old and I was left with the job of cooking for my sister and my dad. Mrs. Archer taught me how to cook and loved giving me tips on what Leon liked best. Now, I guess he can't tell the difference between my food and his mom's. Isn't that just like a man?"

Kacey narrowed her eyes at Nona and silently counted to ten, unsure about how she ought to react to this rather odd revelation. Obviously, Nona was taking great pleasure in flaunting her longstanding friendship with Leon. But why? What was this woman after?

"Uh, yeah. I guess most men are like that," Kacey finally managed, curious to know more about Nona James. She hesitated, drew in a silent breath and then boldly plunged ahead. If Nona wanted to shift the conversation into overshare mode, Kacey certainly wasn't going to stop her. Why not pump this obvious resource on Leon Archer and get all the information she could? Since Nona and Leon shared a history that had deep roots, Kacey planned to dig for gold.

"So, you and Leon used to be *together?* Romantically?" she queried venturing as politely as possible into the subject she had avoided so far.

"Together?" Nona shot back with a knowing chuckle. "Absolutely. We were inseparable all through high school and even for a while after he went off to college in Dallas. That's the only time we've ever actually been apart. He spent four long years at SMU," Nona said, her voice drifting out on a sigh, as if recalling a happier time. "But I stayed right here in Rockport. I was here when he came home," she stated, jutting out her chin. "I'll never leave Rockport. I love this town, and everybody in it," she added, with a determined clench of her jaw.

Kacey stared at Nona, both intrigued and concerned. The woman seemed transfixed, as if she'd entered a world of her own and had no idea that Kacey was even in the room. The transformation was unsettling, making Kacey wonder about Nona James's emotional state. Was she as loopy as she appeared to be or was she putting on an act to impress Kacey? Obviously, Nona wanted Kacey to know that she was close to Leon, but how close was she? Kacey wondered.

The lights flickered, dimmed and then suddenly went out again, signaling the continuation of the blackout. Nona shook her head as if to clear away the fog and gave Kacey a crooked half smile. "Time to get out of here. See you tomorrow…I hope," she said with wry humor. Then she stood and left the room.

Kacey swiveled back and forth in her chair, shaking her head in amazement. Why hadn't Leon told her that Nona had prepared their dinner? What exactly was their relationship all about, she wondered, glancing up when Leon arrived.

"Everything okay?" he asked as he set his flashlight on the edge of Kacey's desk and moved toward her.

"I'm fine," she replied, pushing Nona out of her mind. The last thing she wanted to do right then was start a conversation about his operations manager, who was obviously stuck in the past. What she craved was to pick up where they'd left off, to be cocooned once again in Leon's arms. Having lost her battle of romantic restraint, she was clearly ready to surrender.

"All right, then. Nothing more we can do here," Leon stated. "The power company is on the job. So let's go see what Rockport is all about."

"I'm more than ready," Kacey said, relieved to get out of the dark and eager to spend the day with Leon.

Circling her desk, she approached him, easing into the hazy beam of yellow light that cut the room in half.

"However, the building *is* empty," he informed her in a hushed voice, as if reading her mind.

"And?" she prompted, anticipating the move she so desperately craved and hoped he'd make.

"So that means nobody is around to interrupt."

"Interrupt what?" she taunted, watching him through hooded eyes, her heart thumping crazily in her chest, her body sizzling with unmet needs that he'd awakened the night before.

"This," he whispered, opening his arms to Kacey, who slipped into them and let him hold her in a loose embrace. She marveled at how easily she'd tossed aside her reservations about exploring a blazing-hot romance with a man she would probably never see again once her mission here was completed. However, this might be just what she needed to put some spice in her life and pass the time while she was stuck in Rockport.

Anyway, she had never felt anything like this with Jamal. *And I never will,* she realized, the clarity of her uncomplicated, routine love life blazing white and bright in her mind. For too long, she'd been willing to settle for predictable sex with a predictable man who did not stir her soul, ignite her heart or slick her tunnel of love like an oil well on fire. She'd submerged her true needs to accommodate a situation that had been convenient, but that had definitely run its course. Now it was time for her to explore the hidden side of her heart.

"Where were we before I left you all alone in the dark?" he asked, placing two fingers under Kacey's chin.

"Right about here," Kacey replied, pressing her body

to his, not about to erect any barriers that would interfere with this raw, sexual awakening that he'd stirred inside her. Though shocked by the intensity of her need to be near him, she loved the sensation of isolation and privacy that descended on her as she stood in his arms.

The shower of slow kisses that he traced from her forehead to her temple and over her cheeks, left her silently panting and choked with desire. When he moved his sweet assault down the side of her neck, she responded to his feather-light touches with a low, pleasure-filled groan that let him know he was on the right track. Between a series of soft, sexy pecks that he placed on all her exposed skin, his hands crept downward—moving along her spine until they clasped her buttocks in a firm caress and crushed her soft womanhood into his rigid sex, fusing them together like two pattern pieces perfectly joined at the seam.

Succumbing to his tantalizing move, Kacey opened her mouth and took his tongue deep into her throat, letting his languid thrusts satisfy a thirst for Leon that she felt might never be quenched. As the dizzying current of attraction raced through her veins, Kacey knew Leon Archer had awakened a flame of desire that would not be easily extinguished, a white-hot heat that would have to burn itself out. As his hands roamed her body and her love tunnel pulsed to the beat of her heart, she silently questioned what was happening to her.

Am I head over hells in lust with this man, or head over heels in love?

Chapter 12

"I can see for miles!" Kacey exclaimed, her splayed fingers shading her eyes against the sun. Leaning forward, she peered through the open lighthouse window high above the water and filled her lungs with salty Gulf Coast air, slowly exhaling as she savored the exhilarating sense of floating high in the blue Texas sky.

"That's an old coastal fort over there," Leon said, coming up behind her to point toward a rugged stone building farther down the coastline that had gaping holes in its walls. "According to old-timers who've lived here for generations, the pirate Jean Lafitte and his band of thieves used to hide out in that fort between raids on ships entering the Gulf."

"Really?" Kacey remarked, assessing the mysterious structure more closely. "It looks so small," she added, turning her head ever so slightly, enjoying the slight brush of Leon's breath on her temple.

"Yes, it does look small from here. But if you get closer, you'll see that it's pretty spacious," Leon informed her.

"Big enough to hold all the pirates and their loot," Kacey joked, savoring the spectacular coastal view from atop the restored lighthouse.

"Exactly. We'll go over next time we have a day when we can goof off," Leon decided, linking his arm through hers to guide her to the other side of the tower to check out a different view of the landscape.

"Another day to goof off?" Kacey repeated, giving Leon a skeptical look. "We can't afford to lose any more time. Today…okay, I'll give you this one because of the unexpected power failure. But from now on, I don't plan to do any more sightseeing. I came here to work, not play tourist on vacation."

"Relax," Leon told her. He clucked his tongue, as if admonishing Kacey for taking her assignment too seriously. "You're way too tense. Forget about your job for today. We'll get everything done, and on schedule, too. Trust me. You have nothing to worry about."

His offhand remark made Kacey's temper flare. What was it with Leon and his cool, relaxed attitude? Maybe that's the way folks operated in Rockport, Texas, but in New York, staying on top of—or even ahead of— schedules was vital. However, she had to trust Leon to be good for his word, and so far, he'd kept his promise to show Kacey a side of Rockport that would impress and intrigue her.

After leaving Archer Industries, their first stop had been the historic Fulton Mansion, a beautifully restored

Victorian house located in the resort area of Rockport-Fulton. With its mansard roof and ornate trim, interior gas lighting, flush toilets and other refinements it was one of the most progressive and luxurious homes built in 1877. As Kacey walked through the restored home and its exquisite gardens, she got a glimpse into the lifestyle of an affluent family in early Texas, giving her a new appreciation for the small coastal town and the early settlers who'd chosen to live there.

After leaving the mansion, they ate homemade doughnuts and drank strong coffee at a quaint café built to resemble a true Texas log cabin. The display case at the café offered more information of coastal life in years past.

Next, they drove to Texas's smallest state park: the Port Isabel Lighthouse Historical Park, where they climbed to the top of the beacon-lit tower, which had been destroyed during the Civil War and fully restored in 2000. As the only lighthouse in Texas open to the public, they took on the challenge and climbed all eighty-two feet of the interior spiral staircase to enjoy panoramic views of Laguna Madre and South Padre Island. The trip had been well worth the minor exertion required to reach the top, where fifteen huge lamps and twenty-one reflectors remained mounted and ready for use.

"Now, how about lunch?" Leon ventured as they headed down the spiral staircase that would take them back down to earth.

"Sounds good. I'm starving. What do you suggest?" Kacey asked, content to leave all the decisions up to Leon, who seemed to be enjoying their excursion even more than she was. With each stop they'd made, Kacey had been impressed by the facts and stories that Leon tossed out about his hometown's past, both entertaining and educating her. He told her about his grandfather's decision to come to Texas from Mississippi and how he'd built a small textile factory from bricks made by hand. He had encouraged many of his friends and relatives to move west and work for him, and that among those who came were Nona James's ancestors, who had been friends with the Archers back in Mississippi.

Hanging out with Leon was fun and relaxing. It had been a long time since she'd felt so alive and fully engaged in something so different. Soaking up the past of Leon's hometown filled Kacey with an intense admiration for him and his family. But who was Leon Archer Jr., really? And why was he so obviously romancing her? Simply to prove that he could, or because he truly had growing feelings for her?

Kacey pondered these questions as she descended the stairs, one hand on Leon's shoulder to steady herself. He felt solid and secure, as if he were a man she could trust to be honest with her. So far, she had not brought up the subject of Nona's strange conversation. But if she did, could she trust Leon to tell her the truth? She was still puzzled about the woman who seemed so deeply embedded in his life.

"Only one choice," Leon was saying, bringing Kacey out of her mental musings. "You have to have Buddy Boy's Barbecue for lunch. No one comes to Rockport without eating at Buddy's."

"I'm game," Kacey agreed, looking forward to some real Texas barbecue and all the trimmings.

Leon chose a booth at the back of the restaurant, where it was quiet, secluded and far from the noisy lunch crowd hanging around the bar. As soon as they were served, he laughed at Kacey's reaction to the oversized platter of ribs, chicken and sausage that the waiter placed on the table, accompanied by separate bowls of fries, coleslaw and beans.

"My God! This is enough for a family of four!" she exclaimed, staring at the oval plate mounded with meat.

Leon laughed in understanding. "Yep. Buddy believes in giving his customers their money's worth."

"You were right," Kacey agreed. "Thankfully, we decided to split one order of meat."

"Hey, there are plenty of folks in here who could polish off that platter and then ask for seconds."

"Well, I doubt I'll make a dent in my half."

"Speak for yourself," Leon tossed back, picking up a rib.

Shaking her head in wonder, Kacey simply watched as Leon cleaned a bone with one bite and then wiped his fingers on a paper napkin and grinned.

"That's how we eat ribs in these parts," he said with a wink, picking up another rib, which he held up to Kacey's lips. "Go ahead. Your turn. You gotta clean the bone in one bite," he challenged, a smirk on his face.

Kacey hesitated, gave him a challenging wink and then leaned over. Quickly, she ran her tongue over one side of the rib bone, allowing her tongue to graze Leon's fingers in the process. A flash of heat shot into Leon's stomach and hit him in the groin when she slid her lips over his fingers and clamped them down in a hard pucker that held his hand in place. Without hesitation, Kacey drew his fingers fully into her mouth, using her tongue to tease his hold on the spicy bone as she removed every shred of meat. He froze, eyes riveted on her as she sucked the bone, sucked his index finger hard, and then licked his thumb, stirring the pot of simmering need that was rapidly building in his groin.

Giggling in satisfaction, Kacey finally opened her mouth and released Leon's fingers, as well as the bone, which was totally cleaned of meat.

"That was absolutely delicious!" she exclaimed, rolling her eyes in satisfaction. "How'd I do?"

"Girl, you are too much," Leon laughed, settling back in his seat. With deliberate calmness, he let his eyes linger on Kacey's face, as if trying to memorize her features.

"I'll let you call yourself an adopted Texan, now."

"Gee, thanks. This sure is good."

"My fingers or the 'cue?"

"Both," she replied, giving him a sassy smile.

"Glad you liked them," Leon responded, picking up his fork to dig into his bowl of beans.

Kacey tasted her beans and groaned. "Damn, these are good. You sure called it right," she said, dabbing a French fry into a pool of ketchup.

"I try," Leon replied, knowing he'd called it right with Kacey Parker, too. *If she can suck my fingers like that, just think what she could do to other parts of my body* he mused, knowing just where he planned to take her after lunch.

Chapter 13

"How about a walk on the beach to burn off those ribs?" Leon suggested after they were back in his Corvette, cruising down Main Street with the top down. The warm April sun hit Kacey's face and added to her sense of contentment. After such a heavy meal in the middle of the day, a walk on the beach sounded like a plan.

"I'd love to…but not dressed like this," she remarked, touching the collar of her silk shirt.

"No problem, I can swing by the Seaside so you can change, okay?"

"Okay," Kacey replied, not wanting this free time with Leon to end, because tomorrow it was back to business. There'd be no more days like this, so she might as well take advantage of the situation and enjoy what was left of her rare chance to goof off.

After Leon parked in front of the motel, Kacey got

out and headed inside to change, leaving him sitting in his car as he watched her walk away. His eyes ran the length of her back and lingered on her round tight booty. He could just imagine how she would look naked, in his bed, her brown curls spread out on a pillow, her legs spread open wide and begging him to enter, her generous breasts plump and round, ready to be fondled. His runaway thoughts brought on an arousal that almost made him gasp. At that moment he had only one desire, to make love to Kacey Parker. But would their relationship ever evolve to that point? Was he just teasing himself with the idea of possessing her completely? Or was he inching his way into her heart?

There's only one way to find out. Test her, he decided, fantasizing about holding Kacey naked in his arms, her lips clamped tightly over his as they began the passion-filled journey he'd been searching for so long.

Kacey raced into her room, stripped off her good slacks, her silk blouse and her midheel sandals. She laid out a pair of capris and a T-shirt on the bed—perfect for her walk on the beach. Moving past the mirror, she paused, taking in her semi-nude reflection. In her thong and bra, she was wearing little more than one of her swimsuits. Turning to the left, then the right, she checked out her profile, the thought of modeling swimsuit samples for Leon rushing to mind. He would be looking at her with even more skin exposed, and the thought of his eyes sliding up and down her figure sparked a prickly sensation that brought on a spasm of delight.

She swept trembling fingers over her abdomen, imagining Leon's palms roaming the flat of her stomach, the curve of her waist, inching ever closer to the Brazilian waxed V that bridged her thighs. She drew in a long breath and sighed, imagining how it would feel to be caressed by his hand as he probed parts of her anatomy that had been long untouched. She wanted his large, but tender hands, unhooking her bra and cupping her breasts. She yearned for his full sensuous lips sucking on nipples that were already jumping to attention. She wanted to taste his maleness on her tongue.

At that moment, her only one desire was for Leon Archer to possess her completely and turn her fantasies into reality. But would that ever happen?

There's only one way to find out, she decided. *Test him.*

They walked along the shoreline that bordered Leon's property, where the waves on his private beach lapped at their bare feet and tickled their toes. Kacey collected a pocket full of pretty shells and twisted pieces of smooth driftwood, while Leon collected mental images of Kacey in the sunlight. He marveled at the way the sun created highlights of gold in her thick brown curls. How the wind pressed her T-shirt into the valley between her lovely molded breasts. How the sprinkling of sand on her arms and legs left a sparkly sheen that made her glow in the sunlight.

Without a doubt, she was the most beautiful woman he had ever known and he had no plans of ever letting her escape the paradise he'd been hoping to share with the right woman one day. It had to be Kacey, he was sure of it. Of all the women he'd spent time with, she was the only one who possessed the qualities he was searching for. She was smart, creative, hungry for success and not ashamed to admit it. She was fun to be with, eager to try new things and made his heart go into a crazy dance whenever she hooked him with her sultry brown eyes. She was interested in the process of textile manufacturing, and understood the demands of his profession. And even though they came from very different worlds, they meshed emotionally like grains of sand on the beach.

Today, he'd noticed how impressed she'd been with the history of his hometown, and suspected that she respected small town life much more now than when she'd first arrived. Getting away from the big city had been a good thing for her and a coup for him. Now, all he had to do was find a way to make her stay.

"We'd better turn around and head back to the house," Leon told Kacey when they came to a deep curve in the beach where the sand gave way to a rocky shoreline.

"Right. It is getting late," Kacey remarked turning around to start back. They walked in silence, holding hands while splashing through the shallow water that lazily caressed their ankles. When they arrived at Leon's house, they mounted the steps leading up to the deck.

"Want something to drink?" he asked Kacey, who had moved to the rail and was looking out over the water.

"Sure. Anything cold," she told Leon, who went inside and returned with a glass of cool lemonade.

"This has been so much fun, Leon. Really. Thanks for everything. I'm beginning to feel more at home in Rockport now." A murmured chuckle slipped out, adding lightness to the sincerity of her remark. "But I think it's time to call an end to our day of playing hooky, don't you?"

Leon tilted his head to one side. He detected a reluctant tone in Kacey's words, and was sure she really didn't want to go back to the motel. What was she going to do for the rest of the evening, anyway? Sit in her room and stare at a TV screen? He doubted that she wanted to do that, and he sure didn't want her to leave.

"Our day together doesn't have to end right now," Leon ventured, taking her hand in his. "This has been a much-needed break for me, too. I forgot about work altogether for the first time in months. Kacey, I loved showing you around. Thanks for letting me spend the day with you." He eased along the deck rail, stopping when his thigh touched hers.

"No, thank *you*," she murmured. "You didn't have to do this. With the power failure and the plant shut down, I know you have other things that are more important on your mind than playing tourist guide for me."

"Not true," he told her in a voice that was raw and sincere. "The power company didn't want anyone on the premises while they were working, and my employees got a day off with pay. Win-win for them, and for us, too…right?"

With an incline of her head, Kacey silently agreed.

"I'm not sure if you're feeling the same vibes that are hitting me," Leon stammered, "but, well… Dammit, Kacey. I…I'm *very* attracted to you."

Kacey watched him closely, aware of how difficult it had been for him to utter those words. Her heart was thudding hard and fast. He'd just told her what she wanted to hear, and now that he had, she was frozen with indecision, knowing he was waiting for her reply. Their time together today had created an amazing sense of closeness. He wanted her. He had feelings for her. But was he being honest with her? Did she dare confess what was really in her heart?

"Leon," she started. "I hear you...I do. And I don't know what's going on, either. But one thing is certain— you sure are making me nervous."

He shook his head and gave her a quick brush of a kiss on her cheek. "Don't be nervous," he comforted, tracing his thumb along her jaw. "We're adults. We can talk about our feelings in a rational way, can't we?"

"I guess so, but I'm still nervous about how fast things are moving. I can't deny that I'm attracted to you, too, but my gut tells me to slow down. After all, I won't be here that long."

"All the more reason to take advantage of me now," he joked. "That way you won't return to New York, wondering...what if?"

Kacey slapped playfully at Leon's arm, knowing he was telling the truth. She would forever regret not exploring her attraction to Leon if she let this opportunity pass. "I can't help worrying," Kacey confessed. "This has been a perfect day. A wonderful afternoon. All that history I've learned. Touring the area. A fantastic lunch. Our walk on the beach. It's all so surreal. I don't usually do things like this at home. And never on a weekday. I hate to see it end."

"I told you, it doesn't have to end." *Ever, if you want it that way,* he wished he could add. Leaning over, he kissed her firmly on the lips, pressing home his point as he pressed his mouth to hers.

With a silent moan of relief, Kacey opened her mouth and accepted his tongue, loving the way he flicked it gently back and forth, teasing her entire body with his feathery touch. "I know," Kacey confessed, when the kiss ended. Licking her glossy lips, she toyed with a wind-tangled curl hanging over one eye, keenly aware of what he wanted…to go inside and explore their attraction more deeply, to shift their attraction to a more intimate level. She knew how impulsive and dangerous it would be to go that far with Leon, but it was exactly what she wanted, too.

When he tugged on her hand, she hesitated, eyeing him with caution as a whirl of thoughts tumbled through her mind: *It's time for me to stop fooling myself. Sex with Jamal is not all that I need. A friend with benefits can't satisfy me forever. I want to feel excited, to fall completely into the experience and lose myself in this gorgeous man.*

Kacey was tired of the empty feeling that came over her after she and Jamal got off and then got dressed. She wanted more. She needed to put her whole heart and soul into a sexual encounter that would allow her to let go and explore the unknown side of her pent-up desires.

"If you want me to take you back to the motel, I will," Leon offered.

Kacey's insides were churning like choppy waves in a storm, but she wasn't in the least bit worried about drowning. Her soul ached for Leon's touch, which she knew would keep her afloat and steady the ride.

It's now or never, girl, she told herself, teetering on the edge of the most important personal decision she had been forced to make in years, knowing she was prepared to take the plunge.

"I can stay," she whispered, smoldering eyes now leveled on Leon. "I think I can stay a while longer."

"Good," he replied, slipping an arm around her waist as they headed into the house.

Heart pounding, legs weak with anticipation, Kacey followed Leon through the open patio doors, across his gleaming kitchen and into the dim haven of his seductively themed bedroom. While the paper tigers and lions and giraffes watched in silence from the walls, Kacey and Leon embraced. Their lips locked and held as soon as they reached the foot of his king-size bed. Their arms remained entwined in a natural grip that held them together like two lost hunters who'd finally found each other in the jungle of love. Tumbling onto the wildly colorful animal print spread, Kacey sank into the heat of the moment, determined to quench her thirst for Leon, which had been growing steadily stronger all day.

Letting Leon slowly undress her felt extraordinarily good, and she had no problem helping him shed his clothes in record time. When their naked bodies touched for the first time, Kacey flinched, electrified by the contact. However, she welcomed the flash of the charge that raced through her body and set her heart afire.

Involuntary shivers of need, fueled by arousal, undulated in the pit of her stomach and wound their way into her throat. She gulped back the surge of sexual exclamations that claimed her tongue and crowded her voice. The fragile shell of forced satisfaction, on which she'd relied during sex with Jamal, evaporated, leaving Kacey raw and vulnerable. Floating on a golden wave of passion that carried her sweetly into Leon's arms, she snuggled up against him.

The hint of stubble on his chin contrasted with the soft feel of his hands as he held her in place and brushed his face along her bare shoulder, nibbling his way onto her right breast. The fire he created as he licked and tugged on her nipple spread hotly through her veins. Kacey curved back her shoulders, giving him complete access to pleasure her intensely, which he did, until she could no longer remain silent and cried out in joy. Revved from the thrill of how her body was responding to Leon's delicious assault, she spread her legs and accepted the two fingers that he slid inside her tunnel of love, which was dripping wet with love juices as never before.

Riding his probing touch, she rotated her hips and let him plunge deeper, eagerly preparing for his stiff tool, which had risen up between them. Sleek and tall, it begged for her attention, making Kacey reach down and surround his throbbing erection with a soft caress. Using her thumb, she made tiny circles on the tip, and was pleased to hear Leon's groans of satisfaction, letting her know she was giving him what he wanted. Increasing her pace, she moved her index finger alongside her thumb, rubbing faster and faster, while devouring him with kisses. Too emotion-filled to think of anything other than the indescribable pleasure of being in Leon's arms, she sank into him, releasing all the dormant sexuality that she'd harbored for too long. Her desire to experience all that Leon had to give overrode any inhibitions she may have had about surrendering to his advances.

Leon eased his fingers from her love-slick center and slid them over her pulsing bud, twirling it with a rhythmic touch that took Kacey to the edge. When he stopped and reached into the bedside table for a condom, she tensed, terrified that she was going to lose the sharp edge of desire that he'd created. However, once his protection was in place and he resumed his tender ministrations, she knew he hadn't spoiled the moment she was searching for.

With a swift move, Kacey guided Leon's shaft down between her legs and into her core, struck by the heat of his body as it coursed through her and the size of his member as it filled her up. His hardness jolted her with satisfaction. Clamping her thighs together she savored the feeling of being totally and firmly connected to Leon. With both hands anchored to his broad brown shoulders, she buried her face in his neck and inhaled the sensuous smell of his skin, surrendering totally to fiery sensations that melted her world.

At first, his languid strokes were easy and tender, as if he were entering a narrow passage leading straight to her heart. Then his pace increased to searing thrusts that flooded her body with a white fire that raged hotter with each move. As he rocked her back and forth, she let her sweetness drain over him, slicking them both as they rose higher and higher toward the mutual climax they both sought. She wished she could ride this wave forever, but knew it had to crash down soon. Hanging onto Leon's shoulders, Kacey bucked along with him until a strong gust of need shook her like a stray leaf in the wind that was quickly drawn out to sea. The shuddering surrender that claimed Kacey, hit Leon at the same time, leaving Kacey gasping for air and Leon quivering in relief. Both thoroughly satisfied, yet not quite ready to let go.

Holding on to Kacey filled Leon with the most contented feeling he had ever known. With her head resting on his chest and her arm flung across his stomach, he melted under the weight of her closeness, as well as her trust in him. Tonight, she had trusted him with her heart and her body, leaving him reeling from her decision. He was tempted to pinch himself to prove that he was not dreaming. She'd made love to him with such fiery intensity that he knew he must be doing something right.

Outside, Leon could hear the waves washing gently onto the beach and the quiet wind as it rushed through the palm trees surrounding his house. The serene setting lulled him into a realization of what he had been missing. For too long, his love life had been a series of romantic misadventures with women he met while traveling for business. Hooking up with beautiful women in faraway cities had been exciting, sexually fulfilling, yet devoid of any real substance.

One of the drawbacks of living and working in a small town like Rockport was that he knew everyone, so he had to leave home to find romance, often forming relationships that were short-lived, with little chance of maturing. He could count on one hand the number of women he'd brought home to his beach house in hopes of creating a more lasting bond. None had ever worked out. After a few visits, they usually drifted away, not interested in settling down in his hometown and knowing he would never move away. His family's business, his future, his parents and his ties to the community held him in place, scaring off women he'd thought he cared about enough to broach the subject of marriage. None had loved him enough to stick with him, so his romances had never worked out. As he shifted his eyes to study Kacey's beautiful profile, he wondered why he was fantasizing about this city girl, Kacey Parker, being any different.

Somehow, he had find a way to convince this lovely, sophisticated, creative professional to leave New York and come live with him in his private slice of paradise on the water. He didn't have much time to make his case, but he was damn sure going to give it his best shot.

Chapter 14

Kacey bit her lip in thought as she headed down the corridor toward Bob Truett's workstation, thankful that the power blip was over and the plant was running smoothly again. Yesterday's outing with Leon had been a wonderful, unplanned escape, capped off by the most satisfying sex she had ever experienced, but that was all behind her and would never happen again. Or would it? Her mind kept turning back to their second go-round in bed. That one had been even better than the first. More tender, less urgent, but just as deliciously electrifying. Now Kacey contracted the muscles of her vagina as she walked down the hallway, aware that her bud was still throbbing in the aftermath of her gutsy tryst with Leon.

It had been nearly two o'clock in the morning when he drove her back to her motel, making for an early rise that began with the expected progress call from Ariana. Groggy and impatient to get up and into the shower, Kacey had opted not to tell Ariana about the power failure or the fact that absolutely no progress had been made on the SunKissed production. She didn't want to get Ariana in a tizzy when there was nothing anyone could do. Today, they'd get back on schedule.

"Good morning!"

Kacey stopped in her tracks when Nona rounded a corner at the end of the corridor, stopped and lifted her hand in greeting.

"Oh, hi, Nona," Kacey called back, but when she started to walk past the operations manager, Nona blocked Kacey's path.

"Enjoy your day off with Leon?" Nona asked, giving Kacey a tight smile.

Kacey narrowed her eyes, not surprised that Nona knew about their outing. In a place like Rockport, it was clear that nothing was kept private very long. "Yes, we had a wonderful time," she answered, adding a hint of smugness to her reply.

"Hmm," Nona murmured. "Leon really deserved some time off. I've been telling him for months that he works too hard. Glad he finally took my advice and got away from the factory for a day."

"I'm just happy that he chose to spend his free day showing me around," Kacey boldly countered.

"I heard you had quite a lunch at Buddy's," Nona continued, arching a brow as she squinted at Kacey.

"You did?"

"Oh, yeah. Nothing new escapes people around here. Talking about strangers is actually one of our favorite pastimes. Gives everyone something to do, I guess,"

Nona went on. "Buddy's Barbecue is the place to be seen if you want to make your presence known around Rockport. Everyone knows what you and Leon ate, drank and probably what you talked about, too."

But do they know how we ended our day? Kacey wondered, lifting her chin as she tried to decipher Nona's motivation. The woman was hard to figure out—was she going to be helpful or hurtful to Kacey in the long run? Were her feelings for Leon just overprotective friendship or something else? Kacey wasn't sure what was going on, but she did know that Nona James was far too interested in Leon's private life and Kacey didn't plan to let this woman get under her skin.

"Leon and I really had a ball," Kacey went on in a deliberately cool tone. "He's the best. A great tour guide. He gave me a history lesson, showed me around, treated me to lunch, and our walk on his beach last night was the perfect ending to our day. I stayed at his house so late that I didn't get back to the motel until nearly two o'clock. I'm a bit sleep-deprived…but I'm here!" *You want something to talk about? Well, take that bit of info to your gossipy friends,* Kacey thought, hoping she hadn't made a huge mistake by telling Nona too much.

With a fast roll of her eyes, Nona dismissed Kacey's remark, as if her comment meant nothing.

"Whatever," Nona said, lifting a finger. "What I stopped to ask you was…do you have the backup disk with the adjusted pattern files on it?"

Kacey frowned, sensing trouble. "No, I left everything with Mr. Truett when we finished. Why?" she asked.

"Seems the adjustments you two made on his computer got wiped out during the power failure. His hard drive, including the CAD software, were fried."

"What? You've got to be kidding!"

"Wish I were."

"You can't mean…we've lost *everything?*" Kacey stuttered, as a sinking feeling swept into her stomach.

"Seems so," Nona stated in a tone that seemed awfully casual as far as Kacey was concerned.

"Are you sure Truett didn't save our changes on a backup?" she pressed.

"I don't know why, but he didn't," Nona confirmed.

"This is a real problem," Kacey sighed, incredulous that she now faced another day's delay. "I'd better talk to Leon about this. Where is he?"

"In his office, I suppose," Nona offered coolly.

Turning around, Kacey headed to Leon's office, entering just as he was hanging up the phone.

"Hey. Good morning. You look lovely," Leon greeted Kacey in a devilishly sexy voice. His heart raced at the sight of Kacey looking so professional and sleek in her business attire. Last night, she'd been a completely different person. Loose and wild and totally free. She'd ridden him like a tiger quenching its thirst after a difficult hunt, and he had given her everything he had—and more. He had never pushed himself so hard to fulfill a woman's needs, but he had gone the distance with her and knew he was a goner. He was totally lost in loving her, but he didn't care. This fabulous woman was exactly who he'd been looking for and he planned to hold on to her forever.

"I was just about to come down to see you," he said, looking her up and down in appreciation. "Baby, last night was…"

"Leon…not now, please. We have more important things to discuss," Kacey advised, making sure she closed his door. The last thing she wanted was for Nona, or any employee, to overhear a discussion about her and Leon's sexual tryst.

Leon shrugged, looking contrite, but nodded in understanding.

"So, what's up?" he asked.

"Nona just told me that the alterations Mr. Truett and I completed were wiped out in the power failure."

"Really?" Leon stood, concerned by the worried expression on Kacey's face. "How could that happen? Truett always safeguards designs with a backup."

"Obviously, this time, he failed."

Leon grabbed his phone, punched in a number and asked Truett to come into his office.

Within seconds the head patternmaker arrived, looking wary and nervous as he stood in front of Leon.

"What happened to the SunKissed file?" Leon asked.

"I don't know, Leon. Somehow, it got corrupted. Must have been the power blip that did it."

Kacey groaned in dismay, but held her tongue.

Truett let out a dispirited sigh. "I know, I know I dropped the ball. I never dreamed something like this would happen," he sputtered, sounding contrite.

"So, we've…lost all that work," Kacey verified, her frustration rising. She turned to Leon, hoping he had an answer. "What do we do now?" she asked, holding in her disappointment.

"Start over, I guess," Leon offered.

"But I'm on such a tight deadline. This is awful!"

she said, hoping Steve Hadley hadn't made a mistake by deciding to use Archer Industries.

Silence reigned while everyone pondered the next move.

"I understand your frustration," Leon finally offered. "I wish this hadn't happened, but it did, and now all we can do is move fast to fix the problem and push forward." He focused on Truett. "Pull up the master file and get started on re-creating everything you and Ms. Parker did!"

"Right away," Truett replied, scurrying from the room.

As Kacey watched Truett leave, her heart thudded in her chest. "Is he reliable?" she asked, worried that this might be just the beginning of a series of setbacks.

"Oh, yes, of course," Leon defended. "The power failure wasn't his fault."

"I understand that, but his lack of security is very disappointing," she countered, biting her lip. But as soon as she saw the look of disappointment on Leon's face, she was sorry for making such a comment. The words had just flown out of her mouth before she'd had a chance to think. If Mr. Truett had been working in the garment district in New York, he might be on his way out the door for making such a mistake. But she wasn't in New York. She was in Rockport, Texas, and she trusted Leon's belief in his employee.

"Truett has been with Archer for twenty-seven years," Leon went on. "This is the first time he's ever messed up. He's always been a loyal employee."

A moment of silence slipped past before Kacey dared speak again. If the circumstances had been different, she might have been inclined to walk away from Archer

Industries without looking back, taking the Leeman's contract elsewhere. But redoing the pattern adjustments would only take a few hours, while sourcing a new manufacturer might take days, even weeks. And besides, she was definitely not about to walk away from Leon Archer, especially not after last night.

"All right. Let's get busy, then," Kacey conceded, determined to put the setback behind her. "However," she began, "I'd like to become a bit more involved in all stages of production. Would that be a problem?" She didn't want to sound bossy, but Hadley trusted her to get the job done right, and on time. She was the one who would be held accountable for how every seam was sewn and she planned to make sure there'd be no more delays.

"Absolutely, I agree," Leon replied. "Feel free to observe, and if you have any problems, bring them to me."

"Thank you," Kacey murmured, letting her shoulders sag, realizing how tense she'd become during their exchange.

"We'll work all day...all night if we have to, to get this back on track. All my other clients' projects will be put on hold until SunKissed is finished. We'll make your deadline," Leon vowed.

"I know we will," Kacey agreed, buoyed by Leon's optimistic attitude and the sense that they were a true team, in this together to the end. He understood her position and did not resent her need to take a keener interest in the production. She would focus entirely on the business she'd come to Rockport to do.

But that doesn't mean I plan to stop playing around with Leon Archer, she decided. No way was that possible, because her entire body flushed hot whenever she thought about the way his sleek sex tool had driven her over the edge and into a chasm of longing from which she hoped never to escape.

The next three days flew by in a flurry of activity as all the Archer employees devoted themselves to the SunKissed by Kacey line. Leon watched as Kacey roamed the factory floor and listened with interest when his employees explained each step of the process. He was proud of the way she put them at ease without trying to interfere.

Kacey worked hard to move the SunKissed project along, rushing the new patterns to the cutters as soon as they were finished, and then standing by as they turned swaths of vibrantly colored fabric into the first pieces of the swimsuit line. Whenever a unit did not meet Leon's exacting standards, he asked the operator restitch it until it was perfect. He'd promised to give Kacey his full cooperation and he did not renege on that.

After four days of full-speed-ahead work, the first units came off the production line. They were perfect examples of Kacey's vision and when Leon suggested that the two of them celebrate at his house on the beach, Kacey quickly agreed.

As they drank champagne and discussed the project, the first glass of bubbly heightened Kacey's awareness of how much she loved designing. The second glass reminded her of how much she loved working with Leon. And by the third glass, she was snuggled against him on one of his comfy chaise longues, with her back spooned against his chest, with his arms holding her close. She felt relaxed and happy that they'd come so far so quickly—both at work and in their rapidly evolving relationship.

"We're almost there," Kacey murmured as she snuggled deeper into Leon's arms.

"Yes, we are," he replied, his breath warm against her neck. "You know, I've got the best employees in the world."

"And why not? After all, they have a wonderful boss," Kacey added, turning her head to place a quick kiss on Leon's chin. "And the most handsome." She kissed the tip of his nose. "And the sexiest." Another peck, this time on the cheek. "And the most…"

But she didn't have a chance to finish her next compliment because Leon eased her fully around, captured her lips in a hungry clench and swept his tongue over hers while pressing his rock-hard sex into the softness of her stomach. She melted under his touch when he slipped his hands beneath her blouse to thumb her nipples until she nearly screamed.

"Kacey…" he whispered.

"Um-hmm," she murmured, not really wanting to talk, only wanting to feel and remember every stroke of his fingertips.

"I have something to tell you."

"Um…what?"

"I… I'm sure I'm falling in love with you," he admitted in a voice raw with desire. "Do you…feel the same way?"

"Yes," she whispered without hesitation, sinking into the beauty of the moment as she gazed up into his eyes. "I can't deny it, Leon. I know I'm falling fast for you," she confessed with a sigh that released all the breath from her body. While the weight of his body pressed down on her, Kacey wiggled out of her jeans and then slipped down on her back. Primed to receive him and eager for his touch, she opened herself to him, knowing their troubles were behind them and an exciting future lay ahead. She also knew that, somehow she would fit into Leon's world and bring him into hers.

Chapter 15

The first-run samples, having been created to fit Kacey's perfect size 4 body, were ready for fitting by her second week in Rockport. As the employees closed down their machines and prepared to head home for the day, Kacey made it a point to walk through the workroom and thank each one for doing such a good job under pressure. No one was upset with Kacey. In fact, their responses let Kacey know that they were proud to have pulled off the task assigned to them, and that their Herculean effort had solved Kacey's problem.

"They're perfect!" Kacey exclaimed when Leon presented her with the final units. She turned each piece of swimwear inside out, examining every seam and tuck. "They've done a good job. Carefully crafted and well made."

"Exactly what I expect from my staff."

"Then the next step is the fitting," Kacey said.

"If you want, there's a dressing room on the second floor that used to be the boardroom. We can use it for the fittings. Need any help?" Leon prompted.

Kacey grinned knowingly. "Sure, why not?"

"My pleasure," he replied voice rough with understanding. "But first, I have a few calls to make. Maybe we can do the fittings a bit later?" he asked.

"Sounds good. Let me know when you're ready," she added, giving Leon a quick wave before leaving his office.

Back in her cubicle, she admired the samples again, realizing how wrong she'd been about Archer Industries, and Leon, too. Steve Hadley had been right. This factory turned out fantastic work. It was precisely the right place to produce the SunKissed line, and Leon Archer was the perfect man for her project…and for her.

It was very late in the day when Kacey and Leon finally got together in the boardroom that had been converted into a dressing room. Everyone had gone home and the factory was quiet. Kacey excitedly modeled each swimsuit for Leon, emerging from the changing cubicle to stand half-naked in front of him while he studied, tugged and pinched the small squares of fabric covering her most private, and sensitive, parts. His smug suggestions and unnecessary ministrations did not fool her at all, and his nonstop touches swept her deeper into her attraction for him. Kacey's desire to make love to him grew more intense as each minute ticked by.

Though Leon was supposed to be helping her create the perfect fit for her sexy bathing suits, he was definitely more interested in examining the curves of her body than the straightness of the seams. When Kacey put on the final suit—a sea-green number with a beaded top and a side tie hipster bottom, his fingers strayed from adjusting the line of the top to touch the rise of her breast.

"I'd tighten this here," Leon said, running a finger across the sprinkling of beads on the bandeau bikini top.

"Uh-uh," Kacey mocked her protest with a frown. "That would hide the beads. That little bit of sparkle has to show…very important for the woman who likes glamour."

"You know best," he smilingly gave in. "You're right. It looks too damn good on you to change. And besides, I'd never want to make you unhappy."

"Never?"

"Never," Leon murmured with conviction, easing his hand beneath the stretchy fabric to capture and stroke a nipple.

Kacey shook her head and rolled her eyes. "You're not paying attention, Mr. Archer," she cautioned in a tease.

"Not true. I'm totally engrossed in what I'm doing," he countered swiftly, slipping her strapless top down and onto the waistband of her hipster bottom.

"Engrossed in what? My body or the fit of the swimsuit?"

"Hey, I'm a pretty clever guy. I can tend to both and do a good job, too, don't you think?"

Kacey giggled and dipped her head. "I guess so."

Leon bent to whisper in her ear, "Let me prove it."

Kacey's entire body went on alert as a spiral of

longing tensed her core. "Here?" she questioned in a rough whisper.

"Why not? We're alone. No one else is in the building," Leon assured her as he leaned in and kissed the space between Kacey's perky breasts. "I'd love to fit something other than a bathing suit on you."

"But that's not what we're supposed to be doing," she huskily replied, groaning as his exploration slipped lower.

"But seeing as how we're finished with the swimwear, all that is left is this." He took her hand and guided it to the bulge in his pants.

Kacey smiled, eased her hand down and wrapped her fingers about his hard rod. She tilted her face up to his to accept the kiss that he pressed to her lips while her hand began a steady up and down motion along his shaft.

Intensifying without breaking their kiss, Leon maneuvered Kacey to the worktable at the back of the room. With a sweep of his hand, he cleared the surface of fabric, clothing, scissors and measuring tapes, and then lifted Kacey up onto it. When she spread her legs, he moved to stand between them, pressing himself into the V-shaped opening as his tongue and hands continued their hungry exploration. The urgency of their passion rushed through Kacey and clouded her brain, blocking out all rational thoughts. Teased by his kisses and inflamed by his touch, she wanted nothing more than to abandon herself to the raw surge of longing that radiated inside her. As bursting gusts of desire orchestrated their tangled limbs, Kacey luxuriated in the anticipation of making love to Leon. He had proven that he knew what she wanted and knew how to deliver, and she was primed for more. As she yielded once again to his embrace, she was shocked by the magnitude of her own desire, but hypnotized by his awesome ability to flood her with uncontrollable joy.

Changing his approach, Leon went from feathering his tongue over her chest to licking a line from her belly button to the top of her swimsuit bottom. Using his teeth, he undid the knot on one side tie and jiggled the fabric until it fell to the floor. Fully exposed, Kacey leaned back and groaned when Leon's lips claimed her vibrating kernel of seduction, which he sucked so hard she let out a gasp. Flooded with uncontrollable sensations of a fast-approaching climax, she braced herself on her elbows, held his head in place and urged Leon to take her where she had never gone before, a place from which she hoped never to return.

How could anything be more perfect, she thought as the climactic wave of release struck, sending her shuddering and laughing and crying and quivering over the edge and deeper into Leon s heart.

Chapter 16

After Kacey slipped into his car, Leon shut the passenger side door and walked around to the driver's side. Pausing, he glanced up at the dark Archer Industries sign above his building and blinked. A sigh of contentment slipped out into the night air. He knew he must look like a love-struck teenager: He couldn't stop smiling. His heartbeat raced like a power sewing machine. And his groin remained aflame with need, though he didn't regret holding back from taking Kacey completely. He hadn't come to the office prepared to make love to her, but he sure hadn't wanted to pass up the opportunity to give her what she obviously wanted and enjoyed.

When she'd told him about her relationship with Jamal, Leon had wished he could thank the guy for priming Kacey to appreciate the kind of loving he knew he could deliver—the kind that Kacey deserved. He appreciated her bold moves, her openness about her sexual needs and the fact that she never made him feel uneasy. Loving a woman like Kacey forever was his only desire, and he planned to put all his energy into solidifying their relationship.

I'm gonna do this one right, Leon decided as he got into his car and started the engine.

While at the office, he struggled to maintain a professional distance from Kacey. In a place like Rockport, it didn't take much to start rumors, and he'd already taken a huge risk by staying alone with her in the building after hours. The last thing he wanted was for Kacey to become the butt of jokes or rumors around the plant. He'd never had sex with a woman in his building and the realization of what he'd just done was titillating, but as he drove into the Seaside Suites Motel parking lot and stopped at the entrance, he decided that it couldn't happen again.

He leaned across to open Kacey's door, and was pleasantly surprised when she captured his lips with hers.

"Guess I'll see you tomorrow," she whispered when the kiss ended.

"Right. Tomorrow," he replied, pulling away. He had to put some space between them because if he didn't, he knew anything might happen.

"Now that the fittings are finished, I'll get Linette onboard," Kacey advised, stepping out of the car. She bent down to look in at Leon, resting her arms in the open window.

"Good idea," Leon said, taking Kacey's hand in his.

He kissed her fingertips, gave her a long look and then let her go. "Call me later...if you want."

"Maybe I will," she tossed back before turning around to enter the motel.

Leon sped out of the parking lot and took the long way home, needing time to process everything that was happening, and happening so fast.

Was she using him to satisfy needs that had been bottled up too long? Was she just out for a fling with a country guy so she'd have something to talk about when she returned to New York? Or was she really, truly in love? As hard as it was to think it could happen, Leon felt in his heart that he had finally found the woman of his dreams.

Kacey called Linette right away and filled her in on everything that was going on between her and Leon. "Girl, this assignment is turning out to be a lot more than I bargained for," she said. "The personal stuff is getting real personal, if you know what I mean."

"Trust me, I do," Linette tossed out.

"Everything's all tangled up. We have to work together, you know. It's absolutely crazy! I need to talk to you because things are moving way too fast."

"Says who?"

"Says me! I know I shouldn't be all cozy with Leon, but damn, he's hard to resist. And a really good guy, too."

"And from what you've told me, he has a secret admirer who may not be so pleased with you and him hooking up?"

"Yeah, Nona. The operations manager. I can't get

a fix on her. She seems friendly enough, but there's something about her I don't trust."

"Leave me alone with her for fifteen minutes and I'll get all the answers you want."

"Girl, I don't doubt that," Kacey chuckled, aware of her friend's blunt, inquisitive nature. "So how soon can you come?"

"I can be there late on Friday…the day after tomorrow. Is that okay?"

"Sure. We can do the shoot on Saturday. Hopefully, at the beach because the weather is expected to be very warm."

"Good. Text me directions to the factory."

"Will do. I can't wait for you to meet Leon. He's easy to work with. And he even might have some photo work for you. I was kinda wary about using Archer Industries, but now I'm glad Leon is doing my line."

Linette laughed into the phone. "Hmm. Sounds like he's more interested in doing *you* than a line of swimsuits," she remarked.

"Hey, you may be right. But as long as he produces on both fronts, I'm happy."

"Sounds serious… I'm really looking forward to meeting your new friend. Later," Linette said, ending the call.

"Later," Kacey murmured into the silent phone, anxious to have Linette around to talk to, if only for a day or two.

While she and Leon had been turning her designs into real swimsuits, Kacey had been turning her heart over to the man whose sensual touch was far more dangerous than his power cutters and industrial sewing machines. This feeling of blissful happiness was so strong, and so foreign, it frightened Kacey. *Can it last?* she wondered, sliding down onto the bed to stare at the ceiling and replay every moment of her dressing room love session with Leon.

Chapter 17

The following day went even better than Kacey had hoped and by the close of business on Friday all the adjustments had been made, the first-run samples were complete and she was ready for the photo shoot. When Leon suggested that Linette use the shoreline along his property to photograph the line, Kacey agreed that it would be the perfect background to show off her swimsuits.

Friday afternoon, Linette arrived at Archer Industries with her load of cameras and supplies. She met Kacey with a hard hug, wrapping her well-toned arms around her friend. An avid runner, Linette kept herself in great shape, taking time between jobs to train for marathons, and wore her reddish brown hair in a short sassy style—easy to manage on the road, she said. Her standard dress was cargo pants with lots of pockets to hold her rolls of film, and tight T-shirts that showed off her fabulously fit body.

"Ready to get to work?" Kacey asked as she walked with Linette toward Leon's office.

"Absolutely," Linette replied, following her friend. "I've been pumped about this shoot ever since you told me that it was finally going to happen. Can't wait to see what you've done."

"I think you're gonna like SunKissed by Kacey. As a matter of fact there is one suit in the line that is perfect for you. A two-piece number in cinnamon that'll look great on your hourglass figure."

After a handshake with Leon when Kacey introduced them, Linette cut her eyes at Kacey, indicating her approval.

Now she sees what I've been talkin' about, Kacey thought, giving Linette an imperceptible nod of understanding as they sat down to discuss their schedule for the next day's shoot.

Once all was set, Kacey drove Linette to the Seaside, where she checked into a room across from Kacey's.

While Linette unpacked, the two friends got busy catching up on personal matters.

"He is too damn fine," Linette commented about Leon as she placed an oversized striped shirt on a hanger.

"Isn't he?" Kacey giggled in agreement. "And sexy as hell, too. At the office he tries to be all businesslike and impersonal, but I know how to wear him down," Kacey confessed, going on to add a few more details about her rapidly evolving romance with Leon.

"I'm happy that you've finally found a serious man to date, after wasting so much time with Jamal."

"Yeah, I know. I've been fooling myself. Trying to act like I was happy with Jamal, but now… Whew! I didn't know what I was missing."

"You sure jumped in all the way. I'm proud of you, girlfriend."

"It is moving kinda fast, huh?" Kacey admitted. "But I…you know what? I think we make a good team. In business and other things, too. Maybe, I'm actually in love?"

"That's pretty damn obvious, Kacey. Anyone can see that," Linette dryly observed. "And I can see that Leon is, too."

"Uh…think so?"

"Yeah. But that's a good thing. You need to stop stressin' so much. What's wrong with great sex with a man you have feelings for? Let it all play out, Kacey. Relax and see where things go. Don't overanalyze the situation and wind up blowing it. You two might have a shot at a real future together."

"I wish…but how could that happen? With me in New York and him in Texas? I told you how he feels about this place. Deep, deep, roots. No way he'd ever leave Rockport."

"It'll work itself out if it's meant to be. For now, just enjoy the journey."

Kacey held back from voicing another round of self-doubts, deciding to take Linette's words to heart. If she and Leon were destined to be together, somehow they'd bridge the differences between where they lived and how they loved. It could be done, couldn't it?

Saturday morning dawned clear and warm, offering the perfect day to photograph SunKissed by Kacey at

Leon's beach house. Linette set up her equipment while Kacey put on the first swimsuit of the shoot—a red satin bikini that showed off her curves with a high-waisted thong and a full-coverage triangle top. The gauzy matching cover-up hit her at midthigh, adding a little extra drama to the ensemble.

Leon watched the action from his deck as Kacey took direction from her friend. He was as impressed with Linette's ability to get just the right poses out of Kacey as he was with the way Kacey's swimwear hugged her body in a perfect fit.

Kacey knows what she's doing, all right, he thought, convinced that any woman would look good in that ensemble, no matter what her figure.

As the shoot continued, Leon began to better understand what Kacey had meant when she'd assured him with confidence that SunKissed would fly out of stores. She was right. Once her line hit the retail market, there'd be no stopping her.

Sitting back, Leon watched the action with pride, admiring the swimsuits that his company had produced. There were low, sexy peekaboo cuts. Retro one-piece units that were ultrachic, and bikinis that featured the tiniest of bottoms as well as skirted styles. He ogled plunging necklines and backless suits that showed off Kacey's soft, mounded breasts and her perfect rear end. He gaped in admiration at a monokini in a passion-purple tone that paid homage to Kacey's smooth Brazilian wax.

A leopard print two-piece with a bandeau top and a boy-cut bottom was his favorite. Created out of the imported Naughty Net, it was electrifying on her. When Leon saw her emerge from the water, her nipples and smooth pubic area peeking through the transparent fabric, the sight made him suddenly go hard. Though he tried to keep his attention focused on the swimsuit, it was difficult to concentrate on anything but the woman who was wearing it. With his eyes riveted on Kacey's seductive brown body as it whirled in front of him, he clenched his teeth, remaining perpetually aroused and primed for action.

He liked what he saw for another reason, too. Kacey and Linette worked well together, and the shoot was progressing without a hitch. No drama, arguing, prodding or delays. Linette impressed him as a talented professional with whom he'd love to work again.

After all the swimsuits had been photographed and Kacey was once again dressed in her jeans and a tie-dyed cotton shirt, they left the beach and drove into town for dinner at Buddy's.

"Where are you off to next?" Leon asked Linette, after they'd been seated and placed their orders.

"I'm heading to Chicago. Don't know if I'll leave tomorrow or Monday morning."

"What kind of a job this time?" Kacey asked.

"A catalog for a parents' magazine. Lots of nursery furniture, toys and strollers."

"And crying babies all over the place?" Kacey prompted.

"Yeah, that, too," Linette agreed with a smirk.

"But it ought to be interesting," Leon commented with a laugh. "Guess your work lets you see the inner workings of a lot of different companies."

Linette nodded. "Absolutely. And it's one of the things that keeps me in love with my profession."

"Ever photographed a Texas rodeo?" he asked, hunching over his glass of soda as he pursed his lips.

"No," Linette replied. "No rodeo—Texan or otherwise."

"Well, if you can stick around tomorrow, I'd love to take you...and Kacey to a rodeo. My friend, Freddy Mathews, has a ranch in Smithville and this rodeo will be a big deal. Townsfolk come out in droves, and out-of-towners, too. A lot of the people who work at Archer will be there, and it ought to be a lot of fun."

"Oh? Sounds like something I don't dare pass up," Linette remarked, shifting her attention to Kacey.

With a shrug, Kacey eyed her friend. "Leon mentioned it a few days ago, but I hadn't thought much about it. You wanna go?"

"Of course," Linette quickly replied. Turning to Leon, she asked, "And it's okay to take photos?"

"Absolutely."

"Then I definitely want to see your rodeo."

"Me, too," Kacey decided, looking forward to meeting people outside of Archer Industries who knew Leon. She could learn a lot about a man by getting to know his friends, and right then, Kacey wanted to know everything about Leon Archer's past. How else could she envision a future with him?

Chapter 18

"This started as an all-black rodeo," Freddy told Kacey and Linette as he guided them toward a huge arena where a crowd of rowdy, yelling rodeo fans were screaming at a man who was trying to stay on a bull that definitely didn't want him to succeed. "However, most people don't think of how important that was for blacks in Texas long ago."

"I know that's the truth," Linette commented. "But Bill Pickett invented bulldogging and was a huge rodeo star, right?"

"Correct," Freddy replied, as he motioned for Leon—who'd lagged behind to say hello to one of his mother's neighbors—to hurry and catch up.

"Pickett was one of the most colorful characters in the history of Wild West shows and rodeo circuits," Kacey added to the conversation.

"I see you two young ladies know your black history," Freddy commented with a chuckle, guiding Linette, Kacey and, finally, Leon into front-row seats. As they settled down, they were greeted by warm hellos and expressions of welcome from many of Leon's friends. Clearly, Leon Archer and his parents knew people from all over the area and were well respected, too.

From her up close and personal location, Kacey watched the action in the rodeo arena with her mouth gaping, impressed by the bravery, skill and awesome strength of the riders who struggled to keep their balance on bucking bulls while holding on to a rigging strap with only one hand. From the expressions on their faces, Kacey could tell that the thrill of the ride overshadowed the pain of the fall when they crashed to the ground or were thrown against a barrier by a testy bull.

"Amazing," Linette commented.

"Here's where you see the true test of a cowboy," Freddy replied.

"It must take a lot of work to put this rodeo on," Linette said.

"Yeah, but it's fun. It all started when my granddad decided to host a bull-roping contest on his farm so his friends could have some fun," said Freddy. "Now, we draw close to a thousand people over the weekend, and contestants travel from as far away as California and Oklahoma to join in."

When a Caucasian cowgirl in a flamboyant black-fringed outfit entered the area on a beautiful bay, the crowd erupted in a volley of loud cheers. "Mary Clayton. Very popular," Freddy explained. "She's a town girl. A newcomer to our rodeo, but she's a favorite to win the barrel race."

"What's that?" Kacey asked.

"In the barrel race, cowgirls ride their horses against the clock, making a cloverleaf pattern as they pass by a series of three barrels."

"So it's not just a black folks' rodeo, huh?" Linette commented.

"Nope. Any cowboy or cowgirl who wants to participate is invited to ride here. No exclusions because of race or culture. Everyone is welcome," said Freddy.

"I've gotta get her on film," Linette decided. She stood, lifted her camera to her face and began to snap away as she moved to the edge of the barrier.

Kacey focused on the lively barrel race, her attitude about Texas beginning to soften as she got into the heart-stopping excitement of the rowdy competition. She'd arrived in Rockport determined to hate her foray into small town America, but here she was, having more fun than she'd had in years. In fact, she had not been bored or homesick since her arrival.

Thanks to Leon, she thought. He'd opened her eyes to the pleasant side of life in his hometown, with their peaceful walks along the beach, their explorations of local history and meals in a barbecue joint where she was now greeted by first name. In Rockport, it seemed that folks either knew you, or went out of their way to befriend you. She had not missed the big city hustle—and hassle—at all, and was finding this slower-paced life to be rather sensual, and definitely worth exploring further…especially with Leon.

Kacey pressed her shoulder against Leon's and tilted her head toward him, suddenly wanting to feel him next to her. He gave her a squeeze and kissed her quickly on the forehead. "Having fun?" he whispered in her ear.

"Yes. It's very exciting, but it sure is dusty," she added fanning away a cloud of dust that suddenly surged up into her face when a cowgirl raced past on a beautiful white horse.

"Yeah, but that's part of the experience. Want a soda?" Leon asked.

"Sure. That would be great. Orange, if they have it."

"They do," Leon assured her, easing out of their embrace. "Be right back."

Kacey had just begun to concentrate on the next rider in the arena when Nona slipped into the space that Leon had just vacated.

"Hi," she said to Kacey, who was waving at Linette on the far side of the arena.

Kacey shifted to the side to check out Nona's outfit. She was wearing a red-and-blue-plaid shirt embedded with gold threads, tight black jeans that hugged her sturdy frame and heavily tooled cowgirl boots with metal clips on the toes. A red felt cowboy hat topped off her Western ensemble.

"You look like you ought to be out there on a horse," Kacey remarked, taking in Nona's flashy Western attire.

"Not me. I do ride pretty well, but I have no desire to compete in a rodeo." She paused, lifted her face to the sunshine and grinned. "Leon and I used to ride all the time. We spent hours roaming these parts."

"That's nice," Kacey muttered through tight lips, inwardly groaning. She was sick and tired of Nona's irritating trips down memory lane. Didn't this woman have anything on her mind other than faded, youthful memories of her and Leon's past? Determined not to show her distaste for Nona's remark, Kacey decided to rub in the fact that *she'd* been invited to come to the rodeo with Leon, not Nona. "I'm having such a good time. Leon insisted that Linette and I come out here today. He's been so good about making sure I enjoy myself while I'm here."

"Leon is a very thoughtful man."

"Yes, he is," Kacey agreed.

"But he's not *perfect,* you know?" Nona abruptly countered.

Kacey leveled a puzzled look on Nona, and then shrugged, returning her attention to a petite Hispanic girl on a huge sable-brown horse who was revving up the crowd as she raced around the barrels.

"No one is," Kacey commented, almost to herself.

"That's true, and Leon's had his share of troubles," Nona continued, measuring her words, as if trying to gauge Kacey's reaction.

"Really? Well, I wouldn't know, or care, about his problems from the past," Kacey snapped, irritated that Nona would dare bring up Leon's personal life with her.

"Well, most people around here know all about what happened. In Rockport, nothing is secret for long," Nona said, adopting a cool tone. "I've known Leon forever, and there's nothing I don't know about him."

"Nothing?" Kacey's head whipped around in disgust, exhausted by Nona's obvious prodding. "I doubt that. There are a lot of things I could tell you about your boss that I'm sure you don't know." She was tempted to ask Nona if she knew that Leon had made love to Kacey in the fitting room at Archer. If she knew that he and Kacey had lain, naked, on his private beach while cool water swept over them. That she'd sucked his cock like a hungry person devouring a lollipop. No….she couldn't, but she wasn't going to tiptoe around Nona any longer, either. It was time for Kacey to show Nona her Harlem-street-tough side and set this woman straight.

"Is there a point to this conversation?" Kacey snapped, letting her frustration fly. "I don't have time for your stupid little games, Nona. If there's something you want me to know, spill it or shut up."

A beat. "You don't have to get snippy."

"I'm not being snippy, just real. If you're so tight with Leon, why aren't you here with him, and not me? As you can see, we're together and you're intruding!"

"Well," Nona began as she sidled up to Kacey. "I only came over because I wanted to warn you."

"About what?" Kacey shot back.

"It's Leon. You seem to be getting pretty close to him, but he's much more complicated than you think."

"Most men are," Kacey deadpanned with a roll of her eyes.

"Did he tell you he has a criminal record?"

Kacey did not reply.

"Leon did time in prison."

Kacey squinted in disgust. "If he did time, then I guess he paid for his mistake, whatever it was."

"Ask him about it," Nona urged.

"If he wants me to know, he'll tell me."

"Bet he didn't tell you he's been engaged four times."

Kacey tensed, but pressed her lips together, not wanting to get into a discussion about Leon's love life with Nona.

"He's the local playboy," Nona continued. "Everybody

knows he can't stick with one woman for more than a few weeks. I'll bet he's told you all kinds of things to make you think he cares for you, but, trust me, he's not really interested. Not romantically, that is."

"And how would you know?"

"Because I know him too well. You're not his type."

"And I guess you are?" Kacey sneered, outraged by this woman's impertinent, know-it-all attitude.

"As a matter of fact, yes, I am. He's only spending time with you because you're the new girl in town. He's curious, but your novelty will wear off soon enough. He'll dump you, just as he's dumped all his women when he's through with them. So why don't you back off before you get hurt? My friendship with Leon is a whole lot stronger than anything he'll ever feel for you."

Kacey looked at Nona as if the woman had lost her mind. "Ha! And you call yourself his friend? Does he know that you go behind his back to spread gossip to hurt him?"

"I'm not hurting him. I'm helping him."

"Obviously you don't care *that* much about his feelings. If you did, you'd respect him, and his privacy, don't you think?" Kacey inclined her head toward the end of the bleachers as Leon approached. "Here he comes now. Why don't you tell him to his face what you just told me?"

"I'll leave that for you to do," Nona challenged in a taunt.

"I plan to," Kacey promised, shocked by the odd conversation she'd just had with Nona. But then, most of her conversations with Nona had been rather odd, now that she thought about it.

"Hey, Nona. How's it going?" Leon asked as he stepped onto the riser. "You're looking real Western. I like your boots," he remarked, reaching past her as he handed Kacey a frosty orange bottle.

Nona smiled cattily at Leon and scooted past him, deliberately brushing her mountainous breast against his arm. "It's all good, Leon. Talk to you later." She wiggled her fingers at Kacey. "See you at work. Have fun you guys."

"What were you two talking about?" Leon asked.

"Nothing important," Kacey replied, turning her attention back to the camera.

Though it was hard to do, Kacey held back from discussing Nona's revelations with Leon, deciding not to ruin their outing. Shoving aside the questions that roamed her mind, Kacey concentrated on the stream of rodeo clowns spilling out of a tiny wreck of a car, determined to have a good time.

When the last event wound down, Leon nudged Kacey and cocked his head toward the exit. They both agreed it was time to leave, but Linette wanted to hang around and take more photos of the rodeo riders. When Freddy volunteered to drive her back to Rockport, Kacey was relieved that she and Leon would be alone in the car, where she planned to grill him until she got to the truth about his and Nona's relationship, and a few other troubling matters.

Thankfully, bidding Linette good-bye helped Kacey disguise her rising anxiety. She hugged her friend hard, wishing Linette could stick around a while longer.

"Sure you don't want to meet for breakfast?" Kacey asked her friend.

"No way," Linette answered with a smile. "I'll be long

gone before you even wake up. Got an early flight out of Corpus in the morning. The next assignment calls."

"Well, good luck in Chicago. And don't let all those crying babies get to you."

"I won't," Linette promised with a laugh.

"Gee, I'm so glad you were able to come and help me out," Kacey added as she gave Linette a final hug. "We'll talk...*soon*."

Once Kacey and Leon were on the road back to Rockport, Leon turned to her. "So what do you think about rodeos now?" he asked.

"It was great. Very entertaining. However, I can't say the same about Nona's performance," Kacey quipped.

Leon grimaced, cut his eyes at Kacey and cocked his head to one side. "Performance? What'd she do?"

"It's not what she did, it's what she said," Kacey tossed out, ending her sentence with a loud huff of disgust that told Leon something was definitely wrong.

He tightened his grip on the steering wheel and listened while Kacey recounted everything that Nona had said, his temper rising to the boiling point as she registered her complaints. "I don't know Nona well enough to gauge her motivation, but you do. What's going on with her? "

Leon stared out the windshield, furious with Nona, yet somewhat relieved that she'd provided the opening he needed to talk about a painful period in his past, of which he was very ashamed. Sooner or later he would have had to tell Kacey about the youthful mistake that had been a source of town gossip for years. It had also been a turning point in his life, forcing him to make big changes and grow up.

"First," he began, "don't believe any of Nona's stupid talk. I wasn't engaged four times only once. And it ended when my fiancée left me for another man. Sure, I've dated around and had some fun. But I'm not a serial heartbreaker."

"What about Nona? Why does she act like you two have something going on?"

"Me and Nona?" He sputtered in laughter. "Absolutely nothing. Other than a longtime friendship. She has a way of exaggerating things. Always has. Yes, it's true that Nona and I dated in high school, but I already told you that."

"She must be stuck in high school then, because she seems determined to try to make me believe that nothing has changed since then."

"Doesn't surprise me that she'd tell you I have romantic feelings for her, which I certainly do not."

"Why is she doing that?"

"Jealous, I guess. You see, she's never really had a serious relationship or dated anyone special. She's a loner. Guess I've always felt kinda sorry for her, and I know I go out of my way to pay attention to her."

"Like how?"

"Oh, sometimes I'll ask her to go to a movie or out to eat, just to cheer her up. Kind of like a big brother would do, you know?"

"But don't you realize how seriously she takes your brotherly acts of kindness? She's in love with you!"

"I dunno about that. She's just lonely," Leon defended.

"No, she's just crazy!" Kacey decided. "And dangerous, too. She told me you did time in prison. Did you?"

"Oh, well, about that. Yeah, but it was county jail, not prison. See how she exaggerates?"

"Why were you arrested?" Kacey wanted to know.

Leon quickly struck back with the truth. "I was young. Running with the wrong crowd. I went to the police to turn my friends in when they held up a store, but I got rounded up with the other guys who were involved in the robbery and spent six weeks in county jail." He paused. "That was so long ago. I can't believe Nona would drag that mess out of the closet. I'm gonna have a serious talk with her."

"A talk? I think you ought to fire her!" Kacey threw out. "I don't understand why you put up with her nonsense, let alone keep her on your payroll."

Leon sighed, feeling Kacey's frustration. He was used to Nona and her quirky ways, but not everyone could tolerate her, as he'd learned to do. "It's not that easy to fire her, or any employee at Archer. Nona has worked for my family's company forever. Only job she's ever had. Where would she go if I fired her? How would she support herself? She'd have to leave Rockport to find a new job."

"And maybe find a new life," Kacey mumbled.

"I can't do that to her. She'll be okay."

"Think so?"

"Yeah, I do."

"Then you're dreaming, Leon. You're way too trusting of her."

"Maybe you're too suspicious. Living in a crime-filled city's made you too paranoid. You're always looking for the worst in a person, instead of the best."

"I'm simply being realistic. You're too damn laid-back."

"You're too tense!" Leon threw back, raising one hand from the steering wheel to slap it back down for emphasis.

"That woman is dead set on causing trouble. And when everything blows apart, I don't plan to be around," Kacey vowed.

Leon bit his lip in concern. Kacey was putting him in a difficult spot. How could he choose between alienating a longtime friend and keeping the woman he had grown to love? How had his life gotten so damn complicated, so quickly?

Kacey sat in silence during the remainder of the drive back to the motel. The tension in the car was depressing. Their argument over Nona had spoiled what had been a perfect outing at the rodeo, and Kacey silently fumed. The fact that Leon seemed to accept Nona's rude behavior was disturbing. What was it going to take for him to see how dangerous she was?

When they arrived at the Seaside Suites, Kacey turned and looked at Leon, knowing her feelings for him had been put to the test. Should she disregard the unsettling tales that Nona was determined to tell? Close her eyes to Nona's attempts to live in the past? Trust Leon to handle things? Or should she get out of Rockport and return to New York, leaving this mess behind?

As much as she wanted to untangle herself from this small town muddle, she knew she had to stay until Archer completed the full production of SunKissed by Kacey. Tomorrow, and during the days that followed, she would work with Leon and finish the job she'd come to Rockport to do because she had plans that depended on successfully bringing her designs to market. She couldn't afford to stumble. What about the apartment in midtown Manhattan that she wanted to lease? Her financial freedom? The sense of professional accomplishment she craved? She'd stick it out with Leon because they made a good team and she needed a successful launch of her designs.

Kacey bit her lip. In business, and in bed, they certainly clicked. The sexual chemistry between them was hotter than any Kacey had never known, but was that enough to counter Nona's dogged interference? Would Leon's odd determination to maintain his friendship with her eventually take its toll on his relationship with Kacey? Did Kacey even want to stick with him long enough to find out? After all, she had a swimwear line to produce. A career to protect. Even though she may have found the man of her dreams, she might have to let him go.

After dropping Kacey at the Seaside, Leon drove along the beach road, his spirits sagging as low as the palm fronds swaying on the dark horizon. He knew he was head over heels in love with Kacey, but worried about what she must think of him now. Maybe he shouldn't have gotten so emotionally involved with this city girl. Nona was right about one thing: Kacey would only be around for a few more days. By next week she might be gone. Falling for a sophisticated woman like Kacey could only lead to a broken heart, anyway. Could Nona be right? Was he fooling himself to think that a woman like Kacey could ever fully understand him or his loyalty to his longtime friends, many of whom were his employees? How much would he have to give up if he wanted to keep Kacey Parker in his life?

Chapter 19

On Monday morning, Kacey went straight into her cubicle without stopping by Leon's office to say good morning. She got busy on her computer, desperate to forget about her testy exchange with Nona and the pain of her argument with Leon. Her impulsive affair with Leon had evolved much too quickly, and she'd allowed herself to tumble into an intimate relationship without considering the consequences. There could be no more daydreams about making love with Leon. No more fantasies about escaping the city to live with him in his paradise on the beach. Instead of allowing herself to be consumed by romantic plans that had no future, she was going to focus on the present. And that required a total break with Leon.

Gulping back her disappointment at the way things had turned out on the personal side of her Rockport adventure, Kacey began to read her emails. The first was a message from Steve Hadley. He'd reviewed the photos that Linette shot on the beach and had approved the samples, giving Kacey the go-ahead she needed to finalize production. He'd copied Leon as well, advising him to institute overtime at the plant if he had to, but to proceed quickly with the SunKissed line. Hadley expected to have finished products shipped by the end of the following week.

That means I don't have much time left in Rockport, she calculated, relieved that Hadley's time frame would help her accept the fact that her stay in Rockport was rapidly coming to an end. Kacey had to make sure that nothing interfered with the scheduled delivery of her swimsuits to Leeman's warehouse in New York.

The remainder of the morning was consumed by a phone conversation with Adriana as Kacey went over their marketing plan. And when Leon buzzed Kacey to invite her to lunch so they could talk, she turned him down, desperate for space and time to cool things down between them.

Leon pulled out of the Archer parking lot and headed to Buddy's for lunch. He'd hoped Kacey might join him so they could begin to patch up whatever had gone wrong. Dammit! He'd instituted mandatory overtime for all his key staff members to push the swimsuit project into its final stage. However, instead of feeling elated, Leon was depressed. At least his father would be pleased to know that the plant was running full tilt and smoothly…even though his attempt to woo Kacey Parker had gone terribly off track.

Kacey was barely speaking to him. Nona was acting

very agitated and remote. And even Bob Truett was unhappy with Leon's push to get the SunKissed line finished ahead of all their other projects. Leon was worried about Bob, who had been acting very nervous and edgy lately. When he stormed into Leon's office to complain about his decision to fast-track Kacey's project over other pending jobs, Leon had been surprised by how upset Truett had been. He'd told Leon that Mr. Archer had never called for mandatory overtime for the entire staff, and that he didn't like pushing those who worked under him so hard. Besides, the decision to let pending contracts languish was going to upset valuable longtime clients and hurt business. He told Leon that by creating such an intense atmosphere in the plant that morale would surely fall and accidents were likely to happen. "Leon Sr. would never have treated his employees this way," Truett boldly admonished.

"Well, Truett, you'll just have to get used to my way of doing things," Leon grumbled to himself as he pulled into the parking lot at the busy barbecue joint.

Sitting in his car, he watched people he'd known all his life come and go, his thoughts centered on the first time he'd brought Kacey to the restaurant. It had been a clear, sunny day like this. They'd had an unforgettable time together. But then, they'd had many unforgettable times, hadn't they? He smiled to recall the night at Archer when they were fitting samples in the dressing room and he wound up pleasuring her on the worktable. He could still feel the rush of desire that gripped him during her erotic photo shoot on the beach. And how could he forget the excitement on Kacey's face as she'd watched her first rodeo? During those moments, he had been absolutely certain that his happiness was grounded in a future with Kacey. But now, he wasn't so sure.

With a shake of his head, Leon got out of his car and entered Buddy's barbecue joint. After picking up a chopped beef sandwich and a soda at the counter, he was headed to a table at the back of the dining room when he heard Nona calling out to him.

"Over here," she invited, motioning for him to join her at the table they'd often shared at the front of the eatery. Through reluctant to do so, he knew it would look awfully strange for him to sit alone in the back of Buddy's when, for so many years, he and Nona and Truett had lunched together at their favorite table near the windows facing the street. Though not pleased to have been trapped into sitting with Nona, Leon decided that doing so might give him the perfect opportunity to talk to her about what she'd told Kacey at the rodeo.

"What's going on?" Nona asked casually, as soon as Leon was seated across from her.

What was going on? Leon wondered, thinking back over the past week, recalling how close he'd gotten to Kacey and how much he didn't want to hurt her. Where had he messed up? All he had done was tell her the truth about his past and defend his friendship with Nona. Was that so bad?

Leon cocked an eyebrow at Nona, then took a bite of his sandwich, and followed it with a long sip of his soda. When he finished, he zeroed in on Nona, ready to hash everything out. "What happened yesterday?"

"Yesterday?" Nona replied, sounding confused. She slid back in her seat, eyes beamed at half mast on Leon.

"Why did you tell Kacey all that mess about my past?" Leon demanded.

With a shrug, Nona frowned, hooked her fingers together in her lap and puckered her plum-colored lips. "I just wanted her to know you better. So I decided to tell her about our old times together, kinda fill her in on you and me."

"You and me?" Leon growled in a tightly controlled voice, no longer struggling to hide his anger. He remained stone-cold still for a long moment before he managed to speak again. "What do you mean by that?"

Silence thickened the tension hanging between them as his question settled in. He watched Nona nervously clench her fingernails into her palms, clearly upset by his angry tone. Perhaps he had been too protective of Nona over the years. By befriending her and allowing her to creep so deeply into his and his parent's lives, he'd made her believe that she belonged to him, that he belonged to her, that their lives would forever be emotionally entwined.

Now, Leon knew he had made a big mistake and it was time for a reality check, even if it destroyed their friendship.

Too bad, he decided. *She's gonna answer to me for getting Kacey so upset, and we're going to settle this right now.*

"I wanted Kacey to know that you and I shared a lot in the past, and we're still close."

"Get this straight, Nona. There is no you and me. No *us,* okay?" Leon paced his words for emphasis.

"I…I only wanted Kacey to know how tight we are. How much I care about you," Nona whined, her voice growing smaller with each word, in definite contrast to her outsize presence.

"I do care about you Nona, you know that. But don't talk about our friendship as if it were romantic!"

"I didn't do that," Nona shot back, suddenly jerking forward. "I never said I was your girlfriend or anything like that. I only told her we used to date."

"Yes, we did. But that's ancient history. Stop living in the past, Nona. You've been my good friend for a long time, but don't try to make it sound like you're more than that. Kacey doesn't need to hear about our past... which is *past*. Understand? There's no need go there, okay?"

"So, are you in love with her?" Nona's question was barely a whisper.

Slowly, Leon nodded. "Yes, I am," he admitted. "And I've told her so." He was tired of playing the field, and knew that he wanted to get married and start a family, but only with Kacey Parker.

"So, it's like that, huh?" Nona huffed her disdain, as if mocking Leon's confession.

Leon flinched to see Nona's face suddenly crumple into a contorted frown, her raw disappointment very clear.

With a sniff, Nona went on. "Kacey's nothin' but another notch to add to your belt of broken hearts."

"Not true. I don't plan to break Kacey's heart," Leon vowed.

"Ha! She'll break *yours* first," Nona snapped. "What do you think is gonna happen when she's finished here? She'll leave you and go back to New York where she belongs. A woman like Kacey Parker would never live in Rockport, and even if she did, she'd never love it like you...and I do. Face it, Leon, it'll never work out for you and her."

"That's not for you to say, Nona. I plan to do whatever I can to make it work with her, and I expect you to respect her. Leave her...and me...alone. Got that?"

"That's kinda hard to do, since your mother and father are like parents to me...and your mom expects me to take care of you."

Leon shook his head in frustration. Nona was determined to cling to him via his mother's emotional ties to Nona's family, but that was not going to work. "My mother didn't ask you to do anything for me! Stop twisting her words. I can take care of myself, so please butt out of my life!"

Leon was not surprised to see tears well up in Nona's eyes, run down her face and streak her makeup. He hated to see her cry. Wished he didn't have to be so harsh with her, but she'd crossed the line and he had no choice but to put her in her place.

Nona sent Leon a cutting look, threw her napkin over her unfinished lunch and stood. Leaning low over Leon, with both hands gripping the table's edge, she told him, "I belong here. Kacey doesn't. You're gonna regret putting all your trust in her." Then she turned, swishing her large hips from side to side as she sashayed out of the dining room, leaving Leon exasperated, yet certain he'd done the right thing. His one and only desire was to keep Kacey in his life, and if he had to push Nona under the bus to make that happen, he didn't care.

Chapter 20

Sleep eluded Kacey. In her bed at the Seaside Suites, she tumbled from side to side, twisting her sheets into knots as visions of her time in Rockport swept through her mind. A miserable week had passed since her rodeo outing and the awful argument with Leon, but so much had changed between them. First, for the worse, and then for the better. And now, everything seemed to be moving ahead smoothly.

The fragrant red roses on her nightstand symbolized how far she and Leon had come in repairing their relationship, and with each breath she took, the scent brought him deeper into her heart. She loved Leon and believed him when he told her that he loved her, too. But would it last? Would the things that made them so uniquely suited for each other overshadow the differences that lurked below the surface? Kacey certainly hoped so, because she yearned for the kind of steadfast love that would last a lifetime, bonding her to Leon for eternity.

With a sigh, Kacey let her thoughts slip back to review the hectic, emotion-filled week, still thrilled, but cautious about all that had transpired. Monday had been the hardest day to get through, and she had only managed to do so by remaining in her office all day, and then leaving the factory very early. On Tuesday, Leon flew to Dallas for a meeting with a potential client, so she'd had a full day without worry over how to avoid him. On Wednesday, they'd been forced to dispense with the mutual silent treatment to discuss a glitch in the production of SunKissed, during which they both agreed that the swimsuits looked fine, but the unit packaging had to be revised. By Thursday, Kacey was so miserable she felt ill, and finally relented when Leon invited her to lunch where they apologized to each other for the harsh words they'd flung at one another in the car. And when Friday arrived, and Leon invited Kacey to attend a Texas beachwear trade show in Houston, where they would have to spend the night, she agreed, prepared to put their troubles behind them and get their relationship back on track.

While trapped in Leon's sports car during the four-hour trip from Rockport to Houston, he and Kacey melted all barriers. They discussed their childhoods, how Kacey had launched her career in retail, their hopes, dreams and visions of the future. And neither mentioned Nona James or her erratic personality.

No longer trying to skirt their emotions, they were able to share personal feelings about love, happiness and even marriage. The ease with which they were able to converse about such deeply private subjects cracked the wall of silence and misguided resentment that had hung uneasily between them all week.

When they arrived at the convention hall in Houston, they playfully explored the exhibits and took in all the excitement of discovering new products and sampling new wares. It was as if the tension and silence of the past had never occurred. They left their private troubles behind and enjoyed the trade show—going with the flow as this new stage in their relationship unfolded.

Now, Kacey turned onto her side and pushed her cheek into her near-flat pillow, reliving the delicious make-up sex they'd experienced while in Houston. Even though they'd been all about business while at the trade show, afterward, when he brought her back to the Hyatt Regency Houston, where they were staying, she'd cratered emotionally and invited him to her room.

Discarding their clothes as soon as the door was shut, they succumbed to a sizzling, skyrocketing sexual joining that fed Kacey's seemingly insatiable hunger for Leon. His sensual tongue had entered every orifice of her body and slicked every inch of her skin. His probing fingers set her spirit aflame and melted all resistance to loving him completely. Lying with him as his hands grazed her body with a possessive, yet tender touch, she eagerly returned his kisses, drinking in his presence with soul-drenching gulps.

By welcoming Leon back into her heart, and her body, Kacey had created a new path to the future, where fiery mutual climaxes, gentle returns to earth and a lifetime of love awaited.

Now, Kacey could still feel the shock of their commitment and shivered in its aftermath. Loving Leon left her tingling with satisfaction and ready to admit that she never wanted to let him go. However, neither of them wanted a long-distance love affair. What they wanted was to be together in one place, and to build a life together. But how?

He was such a loving man. He treated her as if she were a precious gift, which he unwrapped slowly and cherished deeply. Even when they had not been on speaking terms, he had continued to treat her with respect, without pressing or prodding her to change her mind about him, but only to understand. He had been right to leave her alone to make her own decisions about whether or not they had a future together. Now, as they went around town, Kacey no longer felt like a stranger, there to do business and move on. She was Leon Archer's woman and he made no effort to hide the fact that he was totally and hopelessly in love with her.

Despite the pressures of her career in retail and their contrasting lifestyles, Kacey was determined to remain optimistic about sharing a future with Leon. With a smothered groan, she closed her eyes and forced back the lump that was growing in her throat. Too soon, she'd have to go back to New York to work with Steve Hadley as Leeman's launched her swimsuit line. But once the product was in stores and selling well, she planned to come back to Rockport, and back into Leon's waiting arms. As hard as it might be, she had to face facts. Sacrificing her city-bound lifestyle to be with the man she loved might be the only solution.

As her mind weighed her options, she realized that the energy-packed streets of New York and the prospect of moving into a new apartment were not so appealing.

She didn't look forward to getting on a plane headed east, leaving Leon behind—with Nona standing in the shadows, gloating. Even though it was hard to admit, Kacey knew Leon would never be happy in New York. He was a country guy at heart, and trying to change him would only court disaster.

Luckily, Nona had kept her distance since their flap at the rodeo, and that was fine with Kacey. As far as she was concerned, the woman was a pathetic figure trapped in a past that kept her company at night because she didn't have a man of her own. Kacey believed Leon when he said that Nona was only a dear friend, but she still worried that his refusal to acknowledge how dangerous Nona's jealous nature could become might be a big mistake.

"I pity Nona, but she'd have to keep her distance from me and Leon if I moved to Rockport," Kacey murmured, knowing it would be hell to live there as Leon Archer's wife as long as Nona James was hanging around. *But she'll never leave Rockport and he'll never fire her. Something had to give. But what?* Kacey wondered as she drifted off to sleep.

Kacey bolted awake to the shrieking sounds of sirens. She sat up in bed and squinted around the room, confused by the blur of flashing red lights that illuminated the windows. Gasping in alarm, she jumped out of bed, yanked up the blinds and quickly saw that the frightening sounds were coming from two fire trucks that had raced past the motel and were speeding down the road. Troubled by the sight, Kacey's heart pounded in agitation as she watched the vehicles disappear into the night.

Rattled by the disturbance, she went to her minifridge and got a bottle of water. After taking a long swig, she slid back into bed, hoping she'd be able to get back to sleep. However, the phone on her nightstand rang before she could lie down. Panicked, she snatched the receiver while checking the clock. At 2:45 in the morning, who could it be?

"Hello?" she ventured, feeling totally disoriented from the sudden jolt that had awakened her in the middle of the night.

"Kacey. It's Leon. There's a fire at the plant. I'm on my way over there now."

"Oh, no! Not a fire!" Kacey shouted in alarm. "I ll meet you there!" she yelled, slamming down the phone as she hurried to get dressed.

Chapter 21

The sight that greeted Leon when he arrived on the scene made his stomach turn over in despair. Three fire trucks were already pouring water onto the crackling inferno when he stepped out of his car and surveyed the scene from across the road, feeling the heat on his face.

Within minutes, local residents, Archer employees and curious passersby began to gather, pulling their cars to a stop on the road across from Archer.

When Leon saw Roger Evans, the county fire chief, actively directing his men as they struggled to get the fire under control, he raced forward, wishing he could dash inside and rescue Kacey's swimwear, which was boxed and stacked on the loading dock, prepared to be shipped. It was all going up in smoke before his eyes. The sight sent tears streaming down his face.

"Stay back," Roger warned, frowning at Leon, who knew the firefighters were doing everything possible to get the upper hand on the blaze, which seemed to grow hotter by the second. When a burst of flames shot high in the air, Leon screamed, "Oh, no! Roger! Any hope of saving the building?" Then he raced as close to the fire as he dared.

"We're trying!" the fire chief yelled back, waving his arm toward Leon. "Don't go any closer, Leon. This is a pretty aggressive blaze we've got here. Stay back. I know you have solvents inside that can really rev this up and make it blow." Then he turned away from Leon and hurried over to help a fireman who was setting up a fourth hose to attack the raging flames.

Leon sagged against the side of his car and watched in stunned silence as the company his family had built slowly turned into a pile of ashes. The only thing that was not engulfed in flames was the Archer Industries sign, rising high in the dark sky atop the two-story building.

When Kacey arrived and slid her arm around his waist, he pulled her to his side and used the back of his hand to wipe away tears that filled his smoke-stung eyes.

"This is awful," he moaned, voice raw with pain.

"A tragedy," Kacey agreed. "Thank God, no one was hurt."

"For real. I'm gonna find out how this happened— count on it," Leon said through gritted teeth while Kacey stroked his back.

It was midmorning when the last fire truck pulled away from the charred shell that had once been Archer

Industries. Chief Evans stayed behind with the arson crew that arrived to determine the cause of the fire. As Kacey and Leon surveyed the damage, they held onto each other—as if afraid that the fire might consume them, too.

Nona, who'd arrived on the scene shortly after Kacey, remained in her car, looking so stone-faced and angry that Kacey wondered if the jealous woman might know something about what happened. However, Kacey held her tongue. All Leon would do is defend his longtime friend, anyway.

Knots of employees who worked at the plant were standing around, shaking their heads and wondering what had caused the fire that had taken their livelihoods away.

"Leon. I need to talk to you!" Roger Evans called out as he emerged from the ruins and approached Leon, who hurried forward to consult with the fire chief.

Kacey hung back by the edge of the road while the two men engaged in what appeared to be a very serious conversation. As she watched them walk around the still-smoking site, her heart raced and her mind whirled with the implications of this disaster.

Everything was gone. All her hard work had gone up in smoke. Though she knew her thoughts were selfish, all she could think about at that moment was finding another manufacturer to start over, so she could get her swimwear into Leeman's by the end of the month. This disaster could not signal the end for her long-held dream. Surely, Steve Hadley would want to go forward, wouldn't he? But what if he didn't? She began to feel physically ill.

* * *

"The fire chief suspects it might have been arson," Leon told Kacey when he returned to where she waited.

"Arson!" Kacey repeated in shock. "Really? Who would do something so terrible?"

"I dunno," Leon replied, shaking his head.

"I hate to say this…but I wouldn't put it past Nona," Kacey now boldly accused. "She'd do anything to see my swimwear line fail."

Leon jerked back a few steps and peered angrily at Kacey. "Don't you dare accuse Nona of setting this fire! She loves this place as much as I do."

"Just thinking out loud," Kacey defended.

"Don't! That's a terrible thing to say! You don't know Nona the way I do."

"I know that Nona James is not a stable woman and it wouldn't surprise me if she'd do something like this, just to hurt me…and for the attention. All…"

"Stop it, Kacey," Leon interrupted, his voice getting louder and angrier by the moment. "You're way off base. Why would she destroy the company where she makes her living?"

"People under pressure have done stranger things," Kacey threw back.

"Maybe in New York, but not in Rockport. Folks in these parts don't do crazy stuff like that."

"Harrumph," Kacey grunted, jerking her head toward Nona's car. "Believe that if you want to, Leon, but if I were you, I'd be over there asking *her* a whole lot of questions."

Leon shook his head in denial, glowering at Kacey. "I can't have this discussion now." He walked a few steps away and then stopped. "I've gotta go over to the sheriff's headquarters to fill out a bunch of papers. He's the one who asks the questions, not me." Leon hesitated, as if steadying his emotions. "I've gotta do all I can to help the fire department figure this out as soon as possible because the insurance company won't come through until every question is resolved."

"Sure, I know. I'm sorry," Kacey relented, realizing that he was under a lot of pressure and she shouldn't have brought his friendship with Nona into the mix. Maybe Leon was right. Maybe Kacey was jumping to the wrong conclusion and ought to trust his judgment. After all, he knew his employees better than she did and it was his problem to solve. "Yeah, you go ahead," she told him, stepping closer, letting him know she was sorry. "I'm going back to the motel to call Hadley. Gotta let him know what happened."

Leon opened his arms and Kacey moved into them as he held her tight. "Forgive me for yelling. I'm sorry," he murmured against her hair.

"Forget it. This is not your fault," she comforted.

"But I feel responsible. Your dream went up in ashes on my watch."

"Yours did, too," Kacey comforted, feeling the rapid beat of Leon's heart against her breast. She knew he was devastated, as he should be. All she could do was be there for him, encourage him to remain positive. At least no one had been hurt. Archer's insurance would kick in so the family could rebuild and go on.

But can I? Kacey worried, dreading the phone call to Hadley that she knew she had to make.

"I'll catch up with you later," Leon told Kacey, giving her a firm kiss on the lips before letting her go.

"Stay strong," she told him, returning his kiss, one hand caressing his cheek.

As Kacey headed across the road, she looked over at Nona, who had been watching her and Leon. "I hope you saw whatever you were looking for," Kacey said in a voice loud enough for Nona to hear. As she passed by Nona's car, Kacey gave the woman a withering look, then got in her car, made a U-turn and headed back toward town.

Chapter 22

The days following the fire passed in a blur of activity, during which Kacey rarely saw Leon, who was swamped with complaints from upset clients, interrogations with the sheriff's office, and calls from his insurance company. He helped his employees file for unemployment—which everyone took except Nona. Leon decided to keep her on the payroll to help him piece together company records that he'd salvaged from the fire. At least many contracts had been safeguarded in the fireproof safe.

When Leon wasn't comforting anxious employees or meeting with the Archer family lawyer, he was relaying messages to his parents through their travel agent because his mom and dad were in the middle of the desert on safari. His dad had given him three directives to follow: First, do not cancel any contracts; let the clients do the canceling. Second, contact American Textile in Houston and arrange for them to finish any pending projects. And finally, Leon was to use the family house as Archer Industries headquarters until everything was resolved.

With his company in ashes, Leon did as his father asked. He successfully arranged for American Textile Manufacturing to take over clients who did not want to cancel their contracts, and set up a temporary office in his father's study. As he and Nona worked through the paperwork nightmare, he quickly saw that the financial loss for Archer was going to be substantial. Even though Archer's insurance would eventually cover most of his losses, getting cash in hand was going to take some time. However, taking care of his clients was his first priority because once Archer was back in business, he hoped they would return.

Under great strain, Leon stayed closeted in his makeshift office with either Nona or Gerald Ayers day and night as they feverishly worked to sort everything out.

While Leon dealt with Archer Industries' problems, Kacey made progress of her own. She asked Hadley not to cancel their agreement with Archer, but to allow Leon to shift the production to American Textile in order to complete her swimsuit line. He agreed to think about it, but ordered Kacey back to New York until the decision was made.

Hopeful that SunKissed could be saved, Kacey packed her bags and prepared to head home, relieved to have Hadley's fragile support. Leon, who wasn't happy to see Kacey go, was at least grateful that the Leeman's contract remained under his control.

On the night before her departure, she went to see Leon at his beach house for a final evening together.

During the drive there, she thought back over all that had happened since her arrival, which seemed like ages ago. She'd never guessed when she arrived in Rockport that leaving would be so difficult, but then she had never thought she'd fall in love, either. Leon was trying hard to be brave about the separation, but she knew he was hurting as much as she was. Hopefully, they'd find their way back to each other before too long. At least, that was what she kept telling herself as the coastal landscape slipped by.

Leon welcomed Kacey with a deep kiss that totally aroused her need for him and made her moan in satisfaction. As his tongue explored hers, she cupped her hands around his tight, hard butt and squeezed, ready to surrender. However, their goodbye session was quickly interrupted when Leon's cell phone rang. Answering it, he scowled, let go of Kacey and went to sit down on one of the canvas lounge chairs on the deck.

"What did you say?" he snapped, voice sharp and hard. "You've got to be kidding!" He covered the mouthpiece and whispered "Chief Evans" at Kacey, who sat down beside Leon on the chaise.

"What's going on?" she hissed into Leon's ear.

He placed a hand on her thigh and answered with a slow shake of his head, as if whatever the fire chief was saying was too incredible to interrupt. "Impossible. I'm shocked," Leon finally stated, sinking back into his chair to stare glumly at the blue-black sky. "Yeah, I can do that, chief. I'll be there first thing in the morning." And then he clicked off.

Running his thumb over the screen of his cell phone, he focused on the floor of the deck while shaking his head in amazement. "That was Rodney Evans, the fire chief."

"Yeah…I know. So what'd he want?"

"The mystery of the fire has been solved."

"Damn! Does he know who did it?"

Leon swung his head back and forth while a stream of air escaped his lips. "Yeah. It was Bob Truett."

"Bob Truett! You've gotta be kidding."

"Wish I were."

"Why? How'd they find out it was him?"

"He confessed." Leon tilted his body forward, gulping back his shock. "The chief said Truett walked into the sheriff's office tonight and turned himself in. He confessed to setting the fire, and he was responsible for sabotaging the electrical grid and the backup pattern disk, too."

"What? But why?" Kacey pressed.

"Evans said Truett was rambling on about how much he missed working for my father. That he didn't like the way I was running the plant. That I was overworking him and he couldn't take the stress. "

"What did Truett do? How'd he start the fire?"

"He placed open containers of cleaning solvents next to the fabric cutting machines and left them running all night. They overheated and started the fire." A pause while Leon sat in stunned silence. "I can't believe he'd rather see the place destroyed than work for me. He could have quit. He was old enough to retire," Leon said, sounding depressed.

Kacey touched Leon on the arm. "Well, at least, the sheriff can close the case, and now you know what happened."

Leon simply nodded.

Kacey bit her lip, took a deep breath and then plunged ahead with what she knew she had to say. "Leon, I was wrong about Nona. I never should have accused her. I'm sorry, Leon."

Leon took her hand and squeezed it. "That's okay. I understand."

"Thanks, because I didn't. She's your friend, and I shouldn't have doubted your trust in her. I'm sorry, really, I am."

"I appreciate your saying that, Kacey. I know this hasn't been easy for you, either. I'm just happy that Leeman's might still go forward with your line with American taking it over."

"Another good thing that will come out of this," Kacey started, "is that Truett's confession means the insurance company can settle your claim."

"Yeah, so I can start to rebuild."

Kacey nodded. "Right. So why don't we focus on the positive side of the chief's news and not dwell on anything sad tonight."

Leon stood, took Kacey by the hand and tugged her to her feet. "Good idea. I'm not about to let a phone call ruin my last night with you. Now, can we pick up where we left off before my cell phone rang?"

"Absolutely. Let's go inside," Kacey agreed in a voice that drifted into a whisper.

After entering Leon's wild–animal themed bedroom, they came together in a tender embrace, gently and deliberately, as if creating memories to last until they could reunite. Not knowing when that would happen added tension to the experience, creating an invisible thread of caution that heightened their anxiety, as well as their drive to seal their commitment.

Fueled by the tormenting prospect of a long separation, Leon used his lips to nibble a path along Kacey's neck, over her chest and onto each breast, fondling her nipples with his slippery tongue. His hands swept her torso and seared her thighs, massaging her silken skin. When he reached the pleasure point between Kacey's legs, she bucked upward, accommodating his fingers, which he slid deep inside to slick her pulsing core. With his other hand he reached over to grab protection, which Kacey helped him open and slide on.

Impatient to have him completely, Kacey gripped his rock-hard manhood and guided it inside, replacing his fingers with what she craved most—the sensation of his rigid rod filling her up, taking her completely and burning itself into her flesh. As she groaned, writhed and moved under the weight of his naked body, Leon transported her to a place where none of their troubles existed. All that mattered was the connection that bound them, the love that they shared and the promise of tomorrow.

Afterward, they lay side by side in his huge bed, wrapped in each other's arms as they struggled to define the shape of their future.

"I don't want you to go," Leon told Kacey, stroking her hair as he kissed her on the forehead.

"I don't want to leave, either, but I have to," she replied, reaching up to cup her fingers around Leon's chin.

He kissed her fingertips, dragging his tongue over her skin in a sensuous sweep. "You don't *have* to go. Not really. Didn't you say that Hadley has already talked with American?"

"Yes," she whispered.

"So why do you need to go to New York?"

"Because I have work to do. I do have a job, remember?" Kacey responded, shifting in Leon's arms to look at him, trembling with longing as his gray eyes penetrated hers.

"Stay here with me for a few more days," Leon begged. "I need you, Kacey. Hadley can manage the production. You don't need to go."

"Yes, I do," Kacey replied, hating to sound so cold, but knowing it was time to return to reality. The dream escape was over, for now, and she had to face the truth. "I can't throw away my career. I worked hard to get where I am, Leeman's has invested a lot in me and Hadley expects results. As much as I'd like to stay, I can't. I have to leave tomorrow."

Leon shook his head and ran a finger along the side of her face, studying her as if trying to memorize her face. "Kacey, I don't know how I'll stand it, being so far from you. I understand why you have to go, but I still don't like it. I wish you would leave New York completely. Live here with me. We'll get married. Rebuild the plant. Start over together. Leeman's can sell your swimsuits and send you a fat check for your designs. Cut ties with them—and the city—and stay."

"I can't do that," Kacey told Leon, edging out of his arms. She got out of bed and started to dress. Looking out his bedroom window, she saw that the full moon had made a silvery path on the surface of the pitch-black Gulf, leaving a shimmering road that seemed to have no end. As her eyes traced the moonlit water, she thought that the pathway resembled the long road ahead that she and Leon faced. Where would it end? How long would the journey last until they reunited? What awaited them on the other side?

"If you loved me, you'd stay," Leon suddenly challenged.

With her back to Leon, Kacey frowned, troubled by his remark, as well as his attitude. Didn't he see how torn she was over her complicated dilemma? No way could she simply walk away from her career. Why didn't he understand?

Whirling around, she faced Leon, irritated that he expected so much from her while giving up so little of himself.

"Why are you making this so difficult for me? Aren't you being a bit selfish?" she pushed back, confused by his inability, or refusal, to realize that she wouldn't dream of bailing on Steve Hadley, who'd gone to great lengths to advance her career as a designer.

"No, I'm not being selfish," Leon countered. "I love you. I want you with me."

"Leon, I love you, too, but I can't be with you now."

"You could…you could stay. You don't have to live or work in New York to be a swimsuit designer."

"Don't you understand what returning to New York means? That's where I earn a living. The city is my home. Where I belong. At least for now."

"You belong wherever you can be happy, and you can't tell me that you're going to be happy if we're apart."

Kacey sucked in a long breath, allowing his words to roam her mind, knowing what he said was true. "You're right…I won't be happy, but under these circumstances

I'm willing to sacrifice my personal happiness to achieve something just as important."

"What?"

"Success in my career."

"Ah…now I see where you're coming from. You choose career over love. Okay, go for it, Kacey. Thanks for letting me know exactly where I stand."

Kacey stared at Leon, shocked by the hurt in his voice. Was she finally seeing Leon for who he really was? A self-centered man with no feelings for things that meant so much to her? With the future of her swimsuit line in jeopardy and Leon's crazy attitude filling her head with doubts, maybe the best thing Kacey could do was return to New York. She wasn't that keen on small town life, anyway.

"I've got to go," Kacey told Leon, now dressed. She reached for her purse. At least she'd didn't have to ask him to drive her to the motel.

Still naked, Leon got out of bed and walked toward Kacey, appearing disappointed and upset. "Not yet," he murmured, reaching out to her. "I hate that I snapped. It's just so damn hard to let you go. Forgive me?"

Kacey nodded, feeling his misery, and knowing how hard it was going to be for them both. "I'd better leave now. Let's use this time apart to think about what we want and how we can keep our lives together."

"I know what I want," he whispered, inching closer to Kacey, his manhood at attention. "I have only one desire, to live happily ever after with you. To love you forever. If I have to leave Rockport and move to New York, I will. I'd sacrifice all I have here to be with you. You know that, don't you, Kacey?"

Kacey swallowed the pain that stabbed her heart to

hear him say those words. "Yes…and everything *will* work out for us, Leon…but we need time to sort this out. Will you give it to us?"

He pulled her hard to his chest and crushed his mouth to hers. "Yes, you know I will. But let's not take too long," he murmured against her neck.

Without a reply, Kacey pulled away, raced out of his bedroom and across the deck, as the sound of waves hitting the shore pounded in her ears and tears of longing filled her eyes.

Chapter 23

Leon spent his days working out plans to rebuild the factory and his nights reflecting on his and Kacey's dilemma. They spoke on the phone every night, but nothing was the same. The strain of their separation was taking a toll. He missed her like crazy but refused to press her about the fate of their relationship, willing to bide his time until her swimwear was in Leeman's stores and selling well, until she had completed the most important step in her new career. Then, they'd make a decision about what they ought to do.

One thing Leon knew: remaining stuck in limbo as precious time slipped away made him feel like a prisoner awaiting his sentence—hoping for the best, but dreading the worse. The situation grew more unbearable every day.

Two weeks after he and Kacey parted, Nona showed

up at Leon's beach house, holding a bottle of brandy and wearing a too-tight tank top that made her nipples stand out like two silver dollars. When she swept inside and started gloating over the fact that now that Kacey was out of Rockport, everything was back to normal between them, Leon's patience snapped.

"You know I care about you...like a sister, Nona," he told her while pacing his kitchen floor. "But I don't want to ever hear you mention Kacey's name again."

"Oh, don't be so sensitive," Nona poo-poohed. "Face it, Leon. She took my advice. She finally realized that you and I shared a past that was too strong to ignore."

"Stop it! Your gossipy tongue and possessive attitude almost ruined my relationship with her. Leave it alone, okay?"

"Almost ruined your relationship? She's *gone* isn't she?" Nona mocked in delight.

"A temporary separation," Leon clarified in a snap.

"Harrumph." Nona braced one hand on her generous hip and cocked her head at Leon. "Temporary my ass. She won't be back. If she loved you, she never would have left."

"That's enough, Nona. I don't need your take on my love life. Whether or not Kacey comes back is not important. We'll be together somehow, even if we have to fly back and forth. We'll get married, I'll rebuild the factory. We could even work together at Archer and create a good life here in Rockport, if that is what she wants."

"You're dreamin', honey." Nona laughed aloud. "That city gal would never work at the factory with you. Not like I did. She wouldn't fit in."

"And I guess you'd make sure of that, huh?" Leon challenged.

"Yeah, I'd do my best to open her eyes to the way things ought to be."

"How?" Leon prodded, wanting to see just how far Nona would go to get between him and Kacey.

"Like this," Nona said, sidling up to Leon to ease her arms around his waist. When she snuggled her head beneath his chin, Leon froze, determined to let Nona hang herself. Feeling her press herself up against his sex sent a spiral of disgust into his stomach and he knew he'd had enough.

"Kacey was right," he told Nona, untangling himself from her tight embrace. He shoved her away. "You'll never see things the way they really are. You're living in the past and you're pathetic. You know what, Nona? I want you to go away and leave me alone."

"You know you need me here. We've still got a lot of records to process, a ton of work to do."

"I don't think so. As a matter of fact, you're fired," he stated, announcing his decision in a calm voice. Saying those words filled him with a sense of satisfaction he had not expected.

"You can't fire me! Your father would never…"

"My father no longer calls the shots, remember? I own Archer Industries, and there's no place for you in the business."

"You've gotta be kidding. What will I do?" Nona whined.

"I have no idea, but I do know Kacey was right. You think you belong to my family, but you don't. You need to get a life, and get out of mine. Go anywhere. I don't care. Just get the hell outta here right now and leave my mother's key on the counter."

When Nona's face crumbled and tears fell from her eyes, Leon grasped for a way to smooth over his decision. He knew his parents' doting affection over the years had played a huge part in Nona's misplaced affection, and he was at fault, too. He had let things slide too long. "Listen, Nona. Archer Industries is gonna be closed for months. Maybe for a year or more. I'll make sure you draw unemployment and I'll give you a hefty severance payment. You could go to Cleveland, live with your sister."

Nona squinted in question at Leon, but let her shoulders drop in resignation. A tremble of a smile began to tease her lips. "How hefty?" she inquired slyly.

Without missing a beat, Leon told her, "Hefty enough to take care of you, *and* your sister for a long time."

"Well...it's your money," Nona quipped as she dug into her purse and pulled out his key. She slammed it down on Leon's kitchen counter. "All right. I'll go, but you'll be sorry," she told Leon, and then she flounced out the door.

I doubt that, Leon thought, feeling a great sense of freedom. He had severed a troublesome link to his past and he didn't feel the least bit guilty about it. His parents were no longer hovering in the shadows, judging his every move. He was in charge and had no one to answer to but himself. Suddenly, leaving Rockport seemed possible, even plausible. He could join Kacey in New York. But if he showed up on her turf, would he fit into her hectic, sophisticated world? And did he really want to live in New York City?

* * *

Kacey stared at Ariana, stunned. "What do you mean, Steve Hadley is out?"

"Yes, darling. Replaced by his younger brother, Paul. You know. The one who used to run the store in Los Angeles."

"Why?"

"I don't know why or how, but Paul Hadley managed to push Steve out and take his place as head of the company," Ariana finished, fluffing her blond hair with one hand.

"Damn, what does that mean for us?" Kacey wanted to know.

"I don't know, but we'll find out soon. Staff meeting at ten," Ariana told Kacey, smiling secretively as she left Kacey's office.

Kacey nervously watched the clock until it was time for the gathering in Leeman's conference room. Sitting there, she recalled her pitch for the SunKissed line and how excited she'd been when Steve had green-lighted her project. Now she sat in the same room waiting for Paul Hadley to decide her fate.

It did not take long for her new boss to confirm Kacey's worst fears. He was canceling all of Steve's pending projects, including SunKissed by Kacey, and was reassigning the staff to new departments.

"Kacey, you'll oversee promotions for the winter collection," Paul Hadley informed her as he went down the list of changes he'd initiated at the company. "Here's your portfolio. Look it over and we'll get together to discuss the trade show schedule and the target audience for the High Mountain ski collection tomorrow." He handed Kacey a thick binder and then turned his attention to Ariana.

Kacey did not hear anything Paul said to her colleagues. Her heart was pounding, her mouth was dry and her insides boiled in resentment. How did this happen? she thought, mad as hell that her beautiful swimsuits would never make it to market. Leeman's still owned the rights to her designs. She was left with nothing! Everything was gone because Steve Hadley's brother had decided to pull the plug on Kacey's future.

Kacey was tempted to throw the winterwear catalog at Paul Hadley and walk out. But she couldn't. She needed her job and had no choice but to let go of her dream just as she'd had to do with Leon Archer.

Chapter 24

Kacey tried to be a team player, but her heart was not in her new assignment. Things did not go well between her and Paul; they did not see eye to eye on any of her concepts. Every meeting they had ended with her compromising her vision to please him, deepening her resentment and increasing the tension in the office.

When she presented him with ideas for a contest to be held at the winterwear trade show, he dismissed her idea as boring and made snide comments about her being out of touch. When she suggested a new retail floor layout, he picked it apart and eventually turned the project over to an intern who'd never designed a retail promotional booth before. And when she failed to turn in her weekly expense report by noon on a Friday, Paul erupted in a tirade, calling her irresponsible and reducing her to tears.

When she fired back with "You have no right to talk to me like that! I just need fifteen minutes to finish my report," he simply told her, "I don't give second chances."

"I'm not asking for one," Kacey boldly countered, sick and tired of Paul Hadley's imperious attitude.

"Good. Because I hate to watch people grovel," Paul snapped back.

"I'd never grovel to you!" Kacey spat out, glaring at him and wondering how far she dared to push her new boss.

"Fine. I hope you never do," he huffed.

"I certainly won't...because...I quit!" The words flew from Kacey's lips before she could stop herself, but once they were out, she wasn't sorry.

Paul's face turned dark red and his green eyes bulged as he stared at Kacey in disbelief. "Fine, then. Clean out your desk and turn in your keys."

Without a word, Kacey did as Paul ordered, and within ten minutes she was walking like a zombie through the lobby of the building, as miserable as she'd ever been in her life.

On the train headed home to Harlem, she tried to convince herself that quitting her job at Leeman's didn't matter. But she was worried. Finding a comparable job in retail was going to be nearly impossible in this depressed economy. Since she'd quit, there'd be no unemployment checks or severance pay to fall back on. All she had was the nest egg she'd accumulated to buy her new apartment, which was now completely out of the picture.

When Leon called Kacey that evening, she acted as if everything was fine, determined to keep the truth from him about her impulsive decision to quit, though she did tell him that Paul Hadley had canceled the Leeman's contract.

"Gee, I'm sorry, Kacey. I know how much you wanted to see your swimsuits in stores. Maybe you could approach another retailer?"

"No. It's not gonna happen."

When he asked how things were going with her new position, she dodged the question, not able to tell him that she'd quit her job. What would he think if he knew she'd folded under pressure, after all her talk about holding on to her job and how much she valued her career? She'd left Leon to protect her career and now everything was gone. She had no man, no job, no swimsuit line in stores—absolutely nothing to show for all she'd given up to fulfill her dreams.

"You don't sound very happy. I want to come to New York and see you," Leon told Kacey in an urgent tone. "I can fly in tomorrow. Take you out to dinner, to a movie and, afterwards, make passionate love to you."

"Oh, that sounds so good, but not now. I'm soooo busy, Leon. This is not a good time," she protested, using a tone that she hoped would indicate how rushed she was.

"But you're always busy. It's never a good time with you. I need to see you, Kacey. I'll only stay a day or two. If I fly in on…"

"Sorry, but I might be out of town. An assignment might come up, " she floundered, choosing her words very carefully, not wanting to flat-out lie.

"Oh, okay, if it's like that. Well," Leon stuttered, deflated. "Yeah, I understand. Call me when you've got some free time that you can spare, okay." Then without saying goodbye, he hung up.

Sitting in the dark, Leon felt his heart shatter into a million pieces. Kacey was pulling away from him, and he didn't know what to do. He couldn't force himself on her. Yet, he refused to let this separation destroy what they'd created together. He had to reach her, convince her that their love was worth fighting for. He had to hold it all together and get through this rough patch without giving up. Walking away was not an option.

"We'll work it out somehow," he told himself, determined not to let Kacey go.

Leon's parents' arrival back in Rockport was not as joyous as Leon had expected it to be. He was happy to see his mom and dad and anxious to hear all about their trip, but the destruction of the factory and the arrest of Bob Truett cast a sad shadow over the family reunion.

Once Leon finished bringing his father up-to-date on where things stood with company matters, he told his dad all about Kacey—even confessing his feelings for her.

"I knew you two were in love when I first saw you together," his father teased, laughing when Leon squinted at his dad in confusion.

"You saw us? How? When?"

Leon Sr. chuckled and tapped the screen of his handheld device. "This little thing kept me in touch with everything that was going on in Rockport while I was away. Do you really think you can hide anything as newsworthy as a love affair with a city girl in a town like Rockport?"

"You mean people here were spying on me? Sending you photos?"

"Yep, and I'm glad they did. Kacey Parker is a beauty, and she seems like a real smart woman, too. The kind of girl I've always hoped you'd settle down with. You can't imagine how many emails and photos of her I got. Almost every day someone made sure to post a tidbit about her…and my son's romantic adventure. Buddy was the worst. Every time you two entered his barbecue joint or walked down Main Street, he managed to snap a photo and email it to me."

"You mean you've known about us all along?" Leon asked, shocked, yet glad that his father liked Kacey. If he planned to marry her, and he definitely did, he wanted his parents' stamp of approval. "Then you must know about Nona. She left town," he added.

"Yes. Maybe it was time for her to go. She wasn't really happy here, and she was missing out on life. No use in hiding behind memories and sticking to the past. I think she'll be happy in Cleveland. I know your mom will miss Nona, but sometimes we have to put the past where it belongs and move on." Rising from his chair, he went to his safe and began to rotate the combination knob. "Now, about Kacey Parker's swimwear line. You said Leeman's *canceled* their plans to manufacture, and did not sign on at American Textile?"

"That's right. It's such a shame. And Kacey can't take the line to another manufacturer because Leeman's owns the rights," Leon added, feeling a punch of failure hit his gut at the thought of how devastated Kacey must be.

"Hmmm, that's not entirely true," his father remarked as he removed a packet of papers from his safe. He zapped his son with a knowing expression, one eye squinted closed. "Son, your girlfriend needs to know something very important. Here, I want you to read this."

"What is it?" Leon asked as he took the sealed envelope from his dad began to read.

"That's an addendum to the original contract for the SunKissed by Kacey swimwear line that I signed with Steve Hadley. Read it over carefully and you'll see what I mean."

Shrugging, as if the legal document were nothing out of the ordinary, Leon scanned it while his father watched. When he finished, a huge smile spread over Leon's face. "Dad. You shrewd old dog. You sneaked *that* into the contract?"

Leon Sr. beamed in amusement and nodded at his son. "I sure did. And aren't you glad I did?"

Leon let out a whistle of a breath, grabbed his car keys off his father's desk and stood. "I've gotta go," he mumbled, hurrying toward the door.

"To New York, I hope," his father called out, but Leon didn't answer. He was already in his car.

Chapter 25

The taxi ride from JFK to Kacey's apartment in Harlem seemed to take forever. As Leon watched the gritty urban landscape slide by, he knew he would never be happy living in a crowded high-rise building, and worried that he might be wasting his time by trying to get Kacey to leave the lifestyle she loved so much. He desperately wanted to see her, deliver his news and bridge the gap that was keeping them from forging a life together, but he was nervous as hell about her reaction.

After paying the taxi driver, Leon shifted his flight bag onto this shoulder and entered the outer lobby of her building. He scanned the address labels on the buzzers, found hers and pressed—his heart throbbing as he waited to hear her voice.

"Yes?" Kacey's sweet voice drifted through the intercom, sending a jolt of hope into Leon, who took a calming breath and then plunged ahead. "It's me. Leon. I have to talk to you."

A short silence before Kacey acknowledged her visitor. "Leon!" A long hush followed her remark. "Why are you here? I asked you not to come."

"I know, but please I have to see you. I have some very important news."

Without a reply, she buzzed him in.

Leon raced through the lobby, into the elevator, and stood with his shoulder pressed against the elevator wall as it ascended to her floor. Once there, he took long strides down the hall to her apartment, where he impatiently pressed her bell.

When Kacey opened the door, he stopped in his tracks and simply looked at her, wanting to drink in the sight of her and refresh his memories of her beautiful face. She was wearing tight stretch capri pants and a loose pink T-shirt, looking as if she'd just finished a yoga class. Leon tightened his lips as silence hung between them, giving Kacey time to adjust to his unexpected arrival. When she stepped aside, he entered, shutting the door with a backhand push. Without waiting for a word of hello, he took her in his arms, leaned in and teased her with a brush of his lips over hers, testing her resistance and measuring his chances of accomplishing his mission. When she melted under his touch and arched into him, Leon devoured her with a kiss that let her know how much he'd missed her.

As she sank more deeply into his embrace, Leon felt reassured. He had done the right thing, coming to New York unannounced. She did miss him. She desired his touch as much as he desired hers. Why had she buried her true feelings beneath a lot of words that meant nothing?

Kacey opened her mouth and accepted the sweep of Leon's tongue as it caressed hers. Pressing her breasts to his chest, her arms tightened around him until she was breathlessly fused to him, feeling as close as two people could get.

Kacey was stunned, but thrilled that Leon had disregarded her request to stay away. She'd missed him terribly, and having him back in her arms was exactly what she needed. With her world spinning out of control, having him at her side was all that mattered. She wasn't alone. She didn't have to face an uncertain future by herself. He'd proven that he would never abandon her or take their love for granted. At this critical time, he was giving her what she needed most: steadfast devotion and love that would last.

When their kiss broke off, Kacey guided Leon over to her black leather sofa. They sank down together, remaining entwined in each other's arms.

"Leon, I've been miserable without you," she started. "Things have gotten so complicated since I came back. There's a lot that I need to tell you."

Leon placed a finger to her lips and shushed her, shaking his head. "I've been crazy without you, Kacey. I know you didn't want me to come and that you're busy with your job, but I couldn't stay away any longer."

Kacey sucked in a long breath, knowing she had to tell him the truth. "I wish that were true."

"What?"

"I wish I were swamped with work, but the truth is, I'm not busy at all." She stopped, shifted more erect in her seat and looked at the floor. "Leon, I have more time on my hands than I know what to do with." She glanced up at him with soulful eyes. "I quit my job. I walked out on Leeman's, and my career."

With a jerk, Leon leaned to the side and eyed Kacey with suspicion. "You quit? Why?" he demanded, shifting to face her. He hooked his fingers together with hers and waited for her answer.

"I just couldn't work with Paul Hadley. He was so demeaning, so rigid. I tried to keep my temper when he yelled at me over a stupid expense report, but I lost it and walked out."

"Good for you," Leon assured her. "You don't have to take crap from a loser like that."

"Right," she agreed, her voice growing stronger as she described her confrontation with Paul and her impulsive decision to sever ties with her employer.

"I know you were devoted to that company. How could Paul disregard all that you had contributed to Leeman's? What a bastard. He could've tried harder to work things out with you."

"No. He wanted to fire me, but I refused to give him the satisfaction. Someone had to go, and it wasn't going to be Paul Hadley."

"I wish you'd told me about this when it happened. You didn't have to go through such hell all alone," Leon stated, his words tinged with irritation. "You should've called me right away."

"And say what?" Kacey questioned. "That you were right all along? That I shouldn't have allowed myself to put such trust in Leeman's? I shouldn't have believed that my career was rock solid?" Kacey swallowed, twisting her fingers together as she grasped for words to explain what she was feeling. "I didn't want you to know that I'd failed."

"You didn't fail," Leon murmured. "Paul Hadley failed you."

Kacey quickly reconnected with Leon, her lower lip trembling as she continued. "I was a bit naive, I guess. I'd convinced myself that a supportive boss, my own swimwear line in stores and my career were perfectly safe. I thought I had everything, but the truth is, I have nothing now."

Leon pulled Kacey to his side, kissed her on the top of her head, and then gently stroked her shoulder. "Not true. You have me," he murmured. "*And* you still have SunKissed by Kacey."

Kacey dipped her head and studied Leon's dark gray eyes. "If only that were true."

"It is," he insisted.

"No, it isn't. Don't you understand? Because I was working for Leeman's when I came up with my line, I assigned the company all rights to SunKissed," Kacey countered.

Easing out of Kacey's arms, Leon reached for his flight bag, which he'd dropped on the floor when he entered. He unzipped the outside pocket, pulled out the contract that his father had given him and unfolded the legal document.

"Listen to this," he began. "According to the terms of this contract between Steve Hadley (Leeman's , Inc.) and Leon Archer Sr. (Archer Industries), all protected rights to the SunKissed by Kacey swimwear designs will revert to Archer Industries if Leeman's cancels its manufacturing contract for any reason after full production has begun."

Kacey stilled, taking in Leon's revelation, chewing her bottom lip. "Even if there's been a fire? Which was ruled arson?"

Leon handed the contract to Kacey. "Yes. My father had Gerald, our attorney, read it over and he agrees. We were willing to subcontract with American Textile to complete jobs in progress to keep the original contract in force. But since Leeman's canceled...they forfeited their rights. There are no exceptions stated here, so your designs do belong to Archer."

"You mean, to you?" Kacey clarified.

"To *us*," Leon whispered, eyes shining in glee.

"I can't believe this," Kacey whispered, rereading the page that held the key to rebuilding her career. In silence, her eyes traced the densely written page, and then a frown came over her face. "Leon! If you knew about this all along, why didn't you tell me sooner?"

"I just found out."

"When?" Kacey probed, beginning to sound upset.

"This morning. Kacey, believe me, I didn't know."

"You sure?"

"Of course. It was all my father's doing. He and Mom returned from Africa yesterday, so I went to see him to discuss my plans to rebuild the plant. He took your contract out of his safe and handed it to me. I was as shocked as you are. He added that clause to the contract, never dreaming it would be so important. Even Gerald, the company lawyer, didn't know about it."

Stunned by this miraculous turn of events, Kacey slumped back on her spine and gazed at the ceiling. "Then this means that..." she started.

"That you can produce your swimsuits with any

manufacturer you choose," Leon finished. "All we need to do is find one and get started."

"This is…incredible," Kacey sighed. "And after you rebuild Archer Industries…"

"You mean after *we* rebuild Archer, don't you?" Leon stressed, sounding both confident and hopeful.

With a grin, Kacey agreed. "Absolutely. We have a lot to do, don't we?"

Settled on the sofa with Kacey at his side, Leon took her hand in his. "The new facility will be a state-of-the-art manufacturing plant," he said. "As soon as it is up and running, we'll gear up production and launch a lot more of your designs," Leon promised, "You know…I've been thinking…maybe your next project should be a collection of swim trunks for men."

As a hint of a smile teased her lips, Kacey considered his remark. "Oh, really? And I can just guess who'll be my model, huh?" she toyed.

Leon grinned. "Who else? I sure wouldn't want some strange, hunky dude parading around half-naked in front of my *wife* wearing a skimpy male thong bikini or skintight Speedo briefs."

Kacey swatted jokingly at Leon, and then rested her chin on her hand, appearing bemused. "Did I hear you right? You did say, your wife, didn't you?"

Leon studied Kacey with hungry eyes. "Absolutely. That is, if you're willing to leave New York and live with me in Rockport, Texas."

Kacey touched Leon's chiseled jaw, smiling to feel the hint of stubble on his chin, knowing how far and long he'd traveled to bring her such important news. Her heart swelling with joy, she told Leon, "I can't think of a better place to start over, with you." Her husky voice was taut with emotion. "You know…that's an intriguing idea… designing a swimwear line for men. But I'm gonna need some serious inspiration," she taunted, reaching for the top button of his shirt.

Leon edged up to Kacey and let her undo his buttons. "Then, we'd better get started," he urged, shedding his shirt to reveal a smooth brown chest and rippling six-pack abs.

"I'm already inspired," Kacey whispered, sweeping both hands over his torso. Closing her eyes, she smiled and rested her cheek on Leon's bare shoulder.

Leaving New York was going to be easy because Kacey knew the unshakable love that she and Leon shared would only sizzle more hotly under a bright Texas sun.

* * * * *

Fru·gal·is·ta [froo-*guh*-lee-stuh] *noun*
1. A person who lives within her means and saves money, but still looks good, eats well and lives *fabulously*

THE TRUE STORY OF HOW ONE TENACIOUS YOUNG WOMAN GOT HERSELF OUT OF DEBT WITHOUT GIVING UP HER FABULOUS LIFESTYLE

NATALIE P. MCNEAL

Natalie McNeal opened her credit card statement in January 2008 to find that she was a staggering five figures—nearly $20,000!—in debt. A young, single, professional woman, Natalie loved her lifestyle of regular mani/pedis, daily takeout and nights on the town with the girls, but she knew she had to trim back to make ends meet. The solution came in the form of her *Miami Herald* blog, "The Frugalista Files." Starting in February 2008, Natalie chronicled her journey as she discovered how to maintain her fabulous, single-girl lifestyle while digging herself out of debt and even saving for the future.

THE *Frugalista* FILES

Available wherever books are sold.

HARLEQUIN®

Have you discovered the Westmoreland family?

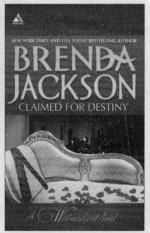

REQUEST YOUR FREE BOOKS!

2 FREE NOVELS
PLUS 2 FREE GIFTS!

KIMANI™
ROMANCE

Love's ultimate destination!

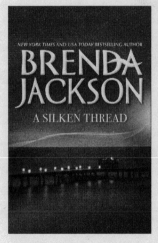